Mira Grant

FINAL GIRLS

FINAL GIRLS

Mira Grant

SUBTERRANEAN PRESS 2017

First Edition

ISBN
978-1-59606-823-0

Subterranean Press
PO Box 190106
Burton, MI 48519

subterraneanpress.com

For Mishell who, like me, would probably enjoy therapy more if it came with a chainsaw.

___ 1. Running.

THE WOOD is dark and the wood is deep and the trees claw at the sky with branches like bones, ripping holes in the canopy of clouds, revealing glimpses of a distant, rotting moon the color of dead flesh. The light it casts turns everything cold and cruel, like something better buried and forgotten. It would almost be better without the moon. They would be running blind without the moon, yes, but at least if they were running blind, they wouldn't have to see.

They run through the skeleton trees hand-in-hand, two girls separated by a handful of years that seemed like an eternity only a few short hours ago (*a few short hours ago, before they were alone in the world; before they were orphans, before they knew the taste of their mother's blood, the glittering trails of their father's tears; before they were everything either of them has left*). Those years don't seem to matter anymore. They hold each other tight. They keep running. They keep running.

They have to keep running.

The scarecrow hunts when the moon is full; that's what the old woman at the library information desk had told them when they'd asked about the quaint local festival their parents had dragged them to. "See to it you don't think you're anything worth the harvest," she'd said, and she'd laughed like a wheat thresher, all loud noises and sharp edges, and they'd left feeling unsettled, ill-at-ease with this strange farming town and its dead-eyed teens, who watched them go with something like hunger and something like hope.

They hadn't known what harvest really was, not then, not there, not when the streetlights were flickering on bright against the gloaming, not when there had been music from the town square and the taste of mulled cider sitting sweet and somehow cloying on their tongues. They hadn't known what it meant to *reap*, to *sow*, to sacrifice.

They think they have some idea now. Understanding is a bitter seed. It can be planted in near to any soil, but water isn't what brings it to bloom. It needs to be fed with other, dearer things, things that, once spilled, can never be replaced.

Things like a mother's heartsblood, red and hot and somehow less than it ever should have been. A mother's love is infinite. Shouldn't her blood, unfairly spilled, be the same?

Things like a father's arms, broken until the bone blooms through the flesh like the petals of some strange, uncultivated flower, a weed growing where it has no business being, fed by screams and accompanied by the sound of muscle tearing.

Things they never wanted. Things they can't forget.

The younger girl stumbles, her foot catching on a root. For a moment, she is falling, suspended in the air, and she knows that if she touches the ground, she is lost, because those are the rules of this strange place, this strange game. They didn't volunteer to play, they didn't ask for this in any way they knew or understood, but here they are, and the game goes on around them, and she is falling, she is falling, she is going to die.

FINAL GIRLS

Her sister's hand catches her wrist and draws her up short, her nose so close to the soil that she can smell its dark goodness, the promise of another season, the promise of rest. Her mother's screams still echo in her ears. It would be...good, to let go, to surrender, to be harvested.

"Diana, come *on*," hisses her sister, and if the soil smells like the future, her sister's voice sounds like the present. It sounds like survival.

"I'm sorry," whimpers Diana. She gets her feet back under herself, and they're running, they're running, they're running together, for the first time ever—the first time in their lives as sisters—they are running *together*, instead of running apart.

The end of the wood looms ahead of them. There is safety on the other side. The scarecrow only hunts within the city limits, and if they can just get over the border—if they can get past the sign that welcomes the unwary to this pastoral slaughtering ground—they'll be free. All they have to do is run.

The trees drop away, and they are running across open ground, through the dry grass that whips at their knees and thighs, grabbing what it can, slowing them down as much as it may. Still they run, and Kim holds fast to Diana's wrist, and they are sisters, they are survivors, they are doing this together. Everything they were before they came here is behind them now, and soon they will be free, soon they will be able to start to heal, soon—

A single long step will carry Kim over the borderline (*it isn't visible, but still she can see it, see it glimmering bright as starlight in the gloom, and she thinks stars are the color of freedom, and she thinks she'll never laugh at the girls who wear glitter eyeshadow again*) when the scarecrow looms out of the dark, as she has always known it would. On some level, she knew that this was all too easy.

She has a second. She has a chance. She has a choice. Let her sister go and let her momentum carry her to safety, or...

Or...

Kim stops running, digging her heels into the soft soil and using the shock of her sudden stillness to catapult her sister over the line, all but hurling her onto the road on the other side of the city limits. The scarecrow howls. Diana screams. Kim smiles and closes her eyes.

"Look away, Di," she says, and she has no doubt her sister can hear her, just as she has no doubt the reaper's blade is rising, bright in the moonlight, black with blood. "S'not a slaughter, it's a sacrifice. S'not murder if you go willingly. Be good. Be good, and look away—"

The knife comes down, silver and rust and terrible.

The world goes to static, and away, taking her sister's screams with it into the void.

>END PROGRAM?

There was something terribly, ironically old-fashioned about the green words blinking on the black screen, a prompt waiting—possibly forever—to be answered. Esther turned a questioning look on the man next to her, resplendent in the sort of white coat she had believed doctors only wore in the movies. Which still might be the case. She was only an observer here, after all, sent to report on this revolutionary new form of therapeutic healing. It would make sense for them to have put their best feet forward, to have donned the scientific equivalent of black tie and tails to make her feel more like they were doing real work here, and not the fringe science equivalent of spinning stories out of fragmented childhood dreams.

(Esther was, perhaps, being slightly unfair in that assessment; she was aware of her prejudices, and of how much care she'd need to take to keep them out of her final report. She was also aware that those prejudices were the reason she'd been selected for this assignment, which was viewed by most of her peers as a privilege she hadn't earned—after all, she was the layman reporter on a staff of scientific experts, the one whose job it was to put hard science into soft words that the casual reader could understand. Her colleagues didn't know where she'd come from. They didn't understand why this was so important. They only knew that she was being given an opportunity many of them would have killed for, and that it wasn't fair.)

"Well?" she asked, when the man didn't reply to her silent question. "Is this where you end the program?"

"This is where we wait," he said, a chiding note in his voice. She wasn't being properly impressed, and it was starting to wear on him. "The program just completed its standard cycle. If there were no errors, and no complications, it will compile itself fully, do a complete physical assessment of the subjects, and release them from their pods."

"The subjects being Kim and Diane Nappe."

"Yes. Ages thirty-seven and thirty, respectively. We get a lot of siblings with a six to eight year gap in their ages—not quite enough for the older sibling to have willingly become a sort of surrogate third parent, not quite narrow enough for them to have felt like they were ever really children together. It's an awkward interval. We help."

"How?"

The question was a barb, designed to sink deep and draw blood when it was ripped loose. The man—the technician—paused before he said, "That's a question for Dr. Webb, I think. I'm just making sure the Nappes wake up from *their* 'nap' without complications." He smiled at his own joke, teeth bright against dark skin.

Esther didn't rise to the cue. "When will I see her?"

"She's currently in an exit review with another group of subjects, which is why we're monitoring the Nappes. She'll be joining us once she's done."

"I was promised full access to the doctor, and I—"

"Believe me, Miss Hoffman, we want you to have it as much as you do. This program has been dogged with misunderstanding and confusion since its inception, and we want the public to understand what we can do here, especially since Dr. Webb is preparing to open a second facility. We looked you up before you came. We know who you are, and we know you aren't inclined to like us."

Esther stiffened. "Is that so?"

"Yes," said the man calmly. "To be honest, that's why Dr. Webb approved your request to document what we're doing here. There's no way your past won't come up at some point during the discussion that follows. It's inevitable. So if you approve of us, we must be legitimate."

"What if I don't?"

"Then we're doing something wrong." He sobered. "I swear to you, we're improving lives and healing wounds that were once thought to be unhealable. We're making the world a better place. If you say we're not, then we're either presenting ourselves badly, or we're all deluding ourselves. Either way, we need to adjust."

"You sound very sure of yourself."

"Because I am."

On the screen, the words disappeared, replaced by INITIATING SCAN. The man's smile blossomed anew.

"There were no issues in the shutdown or the compile. It's scanning them now, and when it finds that both of them have been cleanly disconnected from the virtual environment, it will wake them up."

Instincts honed by years of chasing the story surged to the fore. "Will I get to speak with them?" asked Esther, voice suddenly sharp.

"Not immediately," said a new voice.

They both turned, Esther wary, the man smiling.

"Dr. Webb," he said. "So kind of you to join us."

The woman in the doorway answered with a grin. "I'm always right on time," she said.

Esther had seen pictures of Dr. Jennifer Webb in the promotional material she'd been given to read on the plane, and on the institute's website, where the woman was always posed carefully, artfully, in ways which drew attention to the largeness of her eyes and the kindness of her smile, rather than to the roundness of her waist or the mole low on her left cheek, like a misplaced spot of eyeliner.

In person, Jennifer Webb was short, round, and crackling with the sort of electric energy that came from the passionate, the brilliant, and the hopelessly misled. Esther didn't know which of the three applied to Dr. Webb. It could have been a blend of all of them, one bleeding into the next until they became utterly indistinguishable from each other.

"Hello," she said stiffly, and extended her hand. "I'm Esther Hoffman, from—"

"I know where you're from," said Dr. Webb, not unkindly, and shoved her way between them, taking over the controls. "Looks like our terrible sisters are about to come out of isolation! Let's bring up the view screens, shall we?"

A touch of a button and the floor-to-ceiling screen had become a virtual window on a small, dimly-lit room in which two sealed, gunmetal gray pods rested. There was space around them, sufficient for four more, and blue lights darted around their edges, chasing each other like silvery fish. As Esther and the others watched, the blue lights slowed, stopped, and disappeared altogether. The lights came up in the rest of the room as the pods began to open.

The two women the pods revealed were recognizable as the girls from the horror movie Esther had watched play out on this very screen, but only barely: it was something in the shape of their faces, in the way they wore their bones. They were so much older than the girls she'd seen that it seemed almost like some sort of cruel trick, like she was being shown their mother and her sister, rather than the girls themselves. They were dressed in loose-fitting blue pajamas, with sensors connected to their temples and chests.

"The IVs are part of the pod," said Dr. Webb. "They have to be seated by hand—Charles here takes care of that during the initial descent—but they're extracted automatically when the reification process begins. It's best for the subjects to wake with each other, not with a medical team. This is when we find out whether the therapy has done its job."

"Do they know they're going to be watched?" asked Esther.

"Monitoring at all times is a part of the therapy, and is disclosed in the initial releases," said Dr. Webb. "Unpleasant as it sounds, we even monitor subjects when they visit the bathroom once they're on the premises."

"Because of the overdose," said Esther.

Dr. Webb frowned. "Unfortunately, yes," she said. "We can't allow that sort of situation to arise again."

"Mr. Parker never regained consciousness, if I recall correctly."

"Which you do, or you wouldn't have raised the subject." Dr. Webb shook her head. "Mr. Parker was unable to distinguish our reality, the real reality, from the one we had crafted for his therapy. Upon being told he'd have to live *here*, instead of there, he harmed himself. We've taken steps with our screening and intake procedures, to be sure that sort of thing never happens again."

The two sleeping women's chests rose and fell in a steady rhythm for several seconds before one of them—the elder—took a deep, hitching breath and opened her eyes. She blinked at the ceiling above her, looking confused. Then, with a gasp, she sat up and looked wildly around her, seeming to relax only when she caught sight of her sister.

Slowly, with shaking hands and trembling legs, she pulled herself into a sitting position and stood, tottering to her sister's pod.

"Di?" she said, reaching for her sister's face. She hesitated for a moment before gently caressing her cheek. "Hey, you. Wake up."

Dr. Webb smiled to herself. "Before they started treatment, they could barely stand to look at each other. Kim nearly backed out of the program when she learned her pod would be in a room with her sister's pod, even after we assured them that they'd never have to be awake in the same room. Look at her now."

Esther looked. Kim was studying her sister with concern, protective wariness, and yes, love. It was the sort of love that was virtually impossible to fake, and it was entirely focused on the sleeping Diana.

"Success," said Dr. Webb.

Diana opened her eyes.

She blinked at her sister. Then, sweetly, she smiled. "You got away," she said, and Kim laughed.

Behind the glass, Esther frowned.

"FEAR IS a deep encoder of emotional response," said Dr. Webb. She looked much more credible seated at her big mahogany desk, the wall behind her covered with framed magazine covers and degrees. There was no shortage of academic accreditation around this place. That, at least, had never been in question. No matter how deep Esther had tried to dig, she had never been able to prove that so much as a technician had lied about their qualifications.

"Yes, but how does that justify what some have called 'borderline emotional torture'?" asked Esther. "Surely the risk you're taking with these peoples' minds is more careless than therapeutic."

"I think you have some misassumptions about what we do here," said Dr. Webb. "Will you let me give you the standard spiel, if I let you ask questions about it afterward? That may fix the places where we're not on the same page."

"Or it may not," said Esther. "I assure you, I did my reading before I came here." Not that there was much reading available. The website, the publicity materials, the pieces Dr. Webb had metered out into the world—they were shallow things, never going into sufficient detail to exhaust even Esther's understanding of the science behind the therapeutic techniques. It had taken less time to read everything than it had to fly to the institute's location.

"Humor me."

Esther didn't see a way to avoid it. For better or for worse, Dr. Jennifer Webb was the face of and guiding force behind the Webb Virtual Therapy Institute, bearing the jibes from late-night comedians and unpleasant nicknames with calm, unwavering grace. If Dr. Webb didn't want her there, her article would be dead on the vine, and someone else would get the assignment.

"All right," she said.

Dr. Webb took a deep breath. "As I was saying, emotion is a deep encoder of memory, and fear is especially effective in this regard. Even adults can have their behavior modified on a permanent basis by a deep enough fright. Look at the responses of otherwise well-balanced individuals who've been bitten by an untrained dog. They avoid canine interaction and flinch if a dog comes too near, unless they were, for whatever reason, unafraid of the dog which did the biting."

"They're reacting to the pain."

"Not necessarily. Even individuals who experienced a bite that failed to break the skin due to protective gear or other factors have been known to develop lifelong phobias." Dr. Webb looked at her calmly. "The key is in the interaction between neurochemistry and the body. We experience things with everything we are, not only with our minds. Most therapy focuses only on the mind. We bring the entire person into the process, by creating situations the body will respond to. We create full sense memory, and the associated chemical and emotional responses encode on a much deeper level."

"You mean you're using regression therapy."

There it was: the elephant in the room, the reason Esther had been selected to be the one to come, learn, and report. If she could tell this story without somehow turning it against the institute, it would be because there was no way to give it teeth: no way to show it for the monster she knew, deep down, it had to be.

"No. I never said that. While there are some superficial similarities in the two techniques, they're far from being the same," said Dr. Webb.

Esther narrowed her eyes. "You know who I am."

"Yes," said Dr. Webb. "I do. Esther Hoffman, age thirty-four, pop science reporter for *Science Digest*. You're a debunker. Well-regarded by your peers, well-reviewed in academic journals, with a reputation for an absolutely unflinching dislike of any form of therapy involving the access of supposedly 'repressed' memories. Which is only natural, given what happened to your father. You have my profound apologies, by the way, on behalf of my profession. The people who did that to him...they were no better than charlatans, and frankly, substantially worse in many ways. No one should have that sort of power over someone else's life."

"At least there's one thing we agree on," said Esther, with a forced, chilly calm in her voice. "Regression therapy has been discredited time and time again. The subjects are too easily manipulated, and memory is faulty. Someone who remembers abuse while under the control of a therapist is just as likely to be remembering a dream, or the plot of a television show, as any actual events."

That was the problem. Too many people had come out of regression therapy with false memories, describing devil worship and child sacrifice and other, darker things that were entirely fictions, yet were somehow believed, because they'd been "remembered" under the supervision of a licensed therapist. Like the anti-vaccination lies of the early two thousands, regression therapy had been debunked over and over, yet kept popping up again, a terrible, pseudo-medical hydra that couldn't be killed, no matter how often its opponents tried. Oh, how Esther had tried. She had spent the best years of her life trying, and she intended to keep trying until her dying day.

Dr. Webb sighed. "As I was saying, we researched you before we decided to let you cover this story. There was some concern that your...history...might make it impossible for you to present us fairly. I pointed out that your background would also make an endorsement fully credible. If you say we are what we claim to be, people will believe you."

"Why would you ever think I would do that?"

"Because we're not responsible for what happened to your father, and because if we're successful, we'll present a new way for people to get better, one that doesn't carry the same risks." Dr. Webb sounded perfectly calm, a scientist looking at a rival school of thought and pondering the best ways to blow it entirely apart. "What we do here is not regression therapy."

Esther frowned. "But you said—"

"I said it was similar, and it is. We put our subjects into a hyper-suggestible state, using hypnotic techniques in conjunction with a carefully balanced drug cocktail that blunts the edges of their fear, allowing us to influence them without scaring them to death. Because the scenarios are more real than reality to the subjects while active, we realized early on that we had to be careful to avoid damaging our patients. The drugs help. We use our virtual reality pods—which are a proprietary technology, and which, according to our agreement with your publisher, we are allowed to limit your access to in whatever ways we feel are necessary—to guide the subjects through a tailored, agreed-upon scenario which feels entirely real to them while it's happening, and more importantly, feels entirely real to the body as well as to the mind. Essentially, we rewrite their realities according to their own desires."

"You've been very protective of your virtual reality technology."

"We have competitors attempting to acquire it constantly. That's why we search everyone who comes in or out, and will be making sure you don't leave with any unapproved recordings." Dr. Webb smiled, quick and sharp.

Esther frowned. "That's an insult to my integrity."

"Not with the amount of money some people would offer you for a look at our technology. It would be an insult to assume you were stupid enough to refuse them." Dr. Webb shook her head. "It doesn't matter now. Getting back on the topic, our drugs allow the mind to absorb the shocks we present, while the body's nervous system locks the lessons in place without necessarily writing them to conscious memory. Trauma to the subjects is minimized by careful control of the VR environment and mindfulness training to help integrate the sensory and somatic dissonance of the scenario into waking reality."

"But trauma *is* possible."

"Yes. That's why all scenarios are carefully monitored by our trained technicians, every step of the way, and why we do extensive follow-up with our patients."

"You keep calling them 'scenarios.' Why not admit that you're telling lies?"

"We've never concealed that aspect of our therapy," said Dr. Webb. "We're creating scenarios which *feel* real, which may linger as a vivid but patently untrue memory of a summer night that never was, or a blizzard that isn't in the record books, and which the patients know to be fictional. There will be no trials based on the stories we tell our patients. There will be no ruined reputations. There are signed consent forms describing the scenario to be programmed. There are *logs*. We're telling them lies, and then we're telling them that we told them lies."

"Then why even bother?" asked Esther.

"Because the human mind, while infinitely malleable, forms assumptions and associations, and clings to them tightly, sometimes long past the point of usefulness. Consider the women whose treatment you observed—Diana and Kim. They're sisters, with a seven-year age gap. By the time Diana was born, Kim was comfortably accustomed to being an only child. She resented and avoided her younger sister, viewing every interaction Diana had with their parents as favoritism. As for Diana, she saw Kim as distant and cruel, and never learned to show affection to her sister. Their parents have died. They are the only family they have left in the world, and both of them are hampered by the damage done to their emotional landscapes by their failure to form sibling bonds. So we, with their *full consent*," Dr. Webb stressed the words like they were the only things that mattered in the world—and perhaps they were, "created a situation where they'd need to learn to work together, as sisters. To trust and love and sacrifice for each other, as sisters. The scenario involved a regression to childhood, to access the levels of their emotional landscape where the damage was greatest, and was accompanied by the sort of fixative adrenaline that has shown the most success in making emotional changes permanent."

"You ran them through a horror movie and now they're supposed to be loving sisters," said Esther flatly.

"We ran them through a horror movie and now they *are* loving sisters," said Dr. Webb. "They have three more sessions planned—sequels, if you will—but when their course of treatment is finished, they'll have the sort of strong emotional bond they should have had all along. They may have nightmares, but there won't be any lasting damage in the waking world, because the scenarios we're using are too unrealistic. That's the beauty of what we do here. We change lives without ever creating a situation that could be taken for real."

"I don't believe you," said Esther.

Dr. Webb smiled. "I knew you wouldn't," she said. "If you'd agree to sign a few release forms, I could help you with that."

"Because allowing you to *brainwash* me is the right approach?" Esther scowled. "You must think I'm a fool."

"No. I think you're someone who blames yourself for your father's death, who would do anything to make sure that what happened to him never happens again." Dr. Webb leaned forward. "We don't 'recover' memories. We don't even truly implant them. We modify ways of thinking. We undo damage. We could help you, if you let us—but that's not what I'm proposing. I want you to let me show you that we're not monsters. We just make imaginary ones."

Esther hesitated. "That isn't exactly unbiased reporting," she said finally.

"Miss Hoffman, nothing you did here was ever going to be," said Dr. Webb. "Will you let me show you?"

After a long, long pause, Esther nodded.

FINAL GIRLS

THE PAPERWORK was…daunting, at best. At worst, it was a Sisyphean nightmare designed to keep most people from reading everything they were agreeing to. Esther pinched the bridge of her nose and forced herself to focus, reading every line, looking for the hidden hooks behind the tempting bait.

The room where she'd been tucked away to read and sign her release forms was small and featureless. The walls were glossy white, clearly repainted on a regular basis to keep imperfections from creeping in. The table matched them perfectly, and was bolted to the polished white tile floor at the center of the room. The bolt heads were exposed gunmetal gray, and somehow that little bit of variation made everything around her all the more clinically sterile and unnerving.

The staff files on the facility mentioned that several of the employees came from a theatrical background. A little digging on her part had revealed that they had, each of them, been involved with haunted house design. Several had won awards, placing among the top five percent in the world. And they'd given it all up to come here and rewire the brains of people desperate enough to submit to a half-tested, half-baked idea of therapeutic treatment.

Those bolts were exposed on purpose. They were meant to invoke unease. Esther glared at them, and refused to yield to the psychological design of the room. She was better than these people. She was smarter. She had done her research. They weren't going to break her. They weren't going to beat her. And they certainly weren't going to fool her with something she could buy at the hardware store.

The paperwork was much more frightening. Essentially, she was agreeing to be injected with a complicated, proprietary cocktail of sedatives, hallucinogens, and memory-altering drugs, putting her into a suggestible state that would cause her to accept everything that happened once she entered the pod.

Like hell, she thought. She'd done her share of recreational drugs in college and grad school, and she had never once lost sight of what was real and what was fiction. Reality was a hard habit to quit sometimes, especially for someone who knew what lies could cost.

She would go in knowing who she was, and she would come out the same way, but prepared to tear down everything they'd built here if she had a single unanswered question. She owed it to her father. She owed it to herself. Anything else would be a failure, and Esther Hoffman did not fail. Had not failed since she was fifteen years old, when she'd been unable to save the man she'd loved best in all the world.

If she couldn't save her father, she was going to save everyone else. It was redemption. It was obsession. It was the only thing she had.

There was a knock on the office door. Esther raised her head as the door swung open, revealing a placidly smiling Dr. Webb.

"I brought a few people who wanted to speak with you," she said. "I'm sure you won't mind."

Esther was about to protest—was about to say this was not how these things were meant to be done, that reporting was a process, a series of carefully considered facts strung on a silver wire of narrative, until it could all make sense to the outside observer—when she saw the two women standing behind the doctor. She all but jumped to her feet, sending her chair skittering a few inches back along the tile floor with an unholy screeching noise.

Kim and Diana Nappe, standing patiently, hand in hand, smiled.

"Dr. Webb said you'd like to talk to us about our experience," said Kim, and there was nothing of the hectoring older sister in her tone. She was protecting Diana, that much was clear in every angle of her body and in the way she put herself ever so slightly in the front—not to draw focus or reach for the limelight, but to keep any dangers from reaching Diana before she had a chance to stop them.

Esther wished, briefly, that she'd been able to interview the Nappes before they'd gone into their pods, rather than arriving with their first treatment almost finished. This could be another uncovered bolt, all smoke and mirrors, designed to throw her off the scent of the story. They could be lying.

As she looked into Kim Nappe's eyes, she strongly suspected they weren't.

"Yes," said Esther. "My name is Esther Hoffman. I'm a reporter, working for *Science Digest*, doing an in-depth report on this lab and its techniques. This is the first time the press has been allowed full access, so I'm sure you'll understand why I'm eager to speak with someone who's been through the process. Are you willing to speak with me? On the record?"

"Dr. Webb saved our lives," said Kim. There was absolute conviction in her tone, the conviction of the convert, of the saved, of the survivor who had believed themselves destined to play the victim. Esther blinked, taken aback, as Kim continued, "We're happy to go on the record with you. If we could have done this years ago, we would have."

"Well, no," said Diana, with a warm smile for her sister. "We wouldn't have. We needed to see how bad things could get before we were able to make the effort to help them get better. But I wish we could have done this years ago. I wish we had been strong enough."

"I'll leave you to it," said Dr. Webb, and walked away, giving Esther through her absence the permission to ask the necessary questions. The ones the institute might not want answered.

"Please, have a seat," said Esther, and motioned for the sisters to follow her to the table.

Diana cast a knowing glance at the release forms. "Are you planning to test the process for yourself?" she asked.

"It seems like a necessary part of fair and accurate reporting," said Esther stiffly.

"It is," said Kim. "But maybe lie about your phobias. I can't imagine what would happen to someone who was afraid of spiders." She and her sister giggled as if at some long-standing inside joke, leaning toward one another. They still hadn't released one another's hands.

Esther cleared her throat. "I understand that the two of you chose this procedure in an effort to repair your relationship. Can you tell me what led you here?"

"Oh, no," said Diana. "This wasn't an effort to repair our relationship. We didn't have anything *to* repair. We barely spoke. We couldn't stand to be in the same room for more than a few minutes. When we had to be in the same place, we sniped at each other constantly. We hated each other."

"It was hell," said Kim, matter-of-factly. "I wanted to love my sister. I barely even knew how to like her. Something had to change."

"Why?" asked Esther.

The sisters looked at her with wide eyes, silent and pitying, for several seconds. Finally, Diana said, "Our parents are dead. Did Dr. Webb tell you that?"

"Yes," said Esther. "I'm sorry for your loss."

"I'm sure," said Diana, stiff tone putting a lie into her words. "While our family medical history is none of your concern, we have certain genetic conditions which can dramatically reduce quality of life in later years. Our mother died of one of these conditions. As neither of us is married, it seemed sensible for us to have medical power of attorney over one another."

"But no one gives a sister they hate that kind of power," said Kim. "We're both too smart for that."

"Rewriting your entire personality seemed more intelligent?" asked Esther.

Diana scoffed. "I told you, Kimmie. I told you she didn't really want to listen. Dr. Webb asked us to talk to you," she added, shooting a glare at Esther. "She said you had some preconceptions we might be able to help you with. But you don't want to be helped, do you? You want to sit there and judge us."

"As you can clearly see, my sister is still herself," said Kim, with a fondly long-suffering smile. She patted Diana's hand, and Diana calmed.

A twitch at the corner of Diana's right eye caught Esther's attention. It was like the woman knew, deep down, that the situation was wrong. That she'd been manipulated, changed by forces outside her control. Was the real Diana, the one who would have slapped her sister before yielding for her, still in there?

It was possible this so-called "therapy" worked better for the willing. That would actually be a vote in its favor, strange as that might seem—something that couldn't rewrite the reluctant was much less likely to be adopted by the government as a new form of brainwashing.

Esther took a breath, and smiled. Practice was on her side here: to anyone who didn't know her, it would seem entirely sincere. "I'm sorry," she said. "I didn't mean to give the impression that I wasn't willing to listen. Please. Can you tell me why the decision to rebuild your relationship led you here?"

"It *is* a bit unusual," said Diana, and laughed, a soft, girlish sound that sounded oddly disproportionate coming from her adult face. "We tried the traditional routes. Individual therapy, family therapy, anger management. We even discussed pharmaceutical solutions."

"If there was a pill that could make you love your sister when you didn't want to, we would have found it and taken a handful," interjected Kim.

Diana didn't seem to mind. That was another point in favor of Dr. Webb's technique, however invasive and downright terrifying it might be: Diana was actually smiling when she continued. "We were close to the end of our ropes. We were starting to discuss the possibility of letting it go, just declaring ourselves orphans with no living family and letting the state handle any complications which might arise."

"Meaning they'd unplug us as soon as it got expensive, but still better than giving each other medical power of attorney," said Kim. "It would have been a long, slow form of suicide, and we'd reached the point where we were willing to consider it."

"What changed?" asked Esther.

The sisters exchanged a look. "Don't laugh," said Diana defensively.

"I assure you, I'm not laughing," said Esther. "Please. If I'm going to report about this fairly, I need to know everything."

"I've always been a horror fan," said Kim. She and Diana exchanged another glance. This time, it was Diana who touched Kim's hand, lending her sister just that fragment of resolve. Kim took a deep breath, and said, "I went to a local horror con. They're fun, you know? Meet a couple of B-list celebrities, get some books signed, maybe buy a T-shirt. Dr. Webb was there, giving a talk on how she developed her software, how she put together the therapeutic scenarios, everything."

"When we were kids, the only thing we could agree on was that Saturday night was horror movie night," said Diana. "All the basic cable channels had something with blood and gore and screaming. We'd sit on the couch, and share our popcorn, and feel almost like we liked each other. Like we were...like we were..."

"Sisters," breathed Kim.

The rest of the story was so simple that Esther could have written it without talking to them. It followed the expected beats: it contained nothing new, no dark, unexpected secrets that would cast the whole thing into a new light. Esther would have been happier if it had. At least then, she could have understood how two women, lost without the anchors of their parents, could spin a shared love of horror movies into a reason to rebuild themselves from the ground up rather than keep working through conventional means. Instead, she was left with someone who had seen a...a fringe scientist at best, and a quack at worst, speak surrounded by men in rubber masks and women in bloody lingerie, and had thought "yes, she can save us."

But Dr. Webb had made good on her promises. Despite the shadows in Diana's eyes, she'd agreed to go along with the procedure, hadn't she? After another few sessions, Esther had little doubt those shadows would be gone. The sisters would have each other, forever. It was the cost that had yet to be revealed.

"Do you have any regrets?" Esther asked.

There was that shadow again, sliding across Diana's face like a cloud moving in front of the moon. She put her hand over Kim's, and squeezed, and laughed nervously.

"I don't think I'll ever go to a corn maze again," she said.

___ 2. Hunting.

"DID YOU get the files?" The phone was a heavy weight in her hand, old-fashioned, neither connected to the internet nor capable of communicating with her headset. One of the Institute's long list of restrictions had involved limiting photography and recording devices, as well as access to the local wireless. Esther had a camera that weighed as much as a brick, an internet connection that traveled through more firewalls than the NSA would have demanded, and a phone that was only good for making calls, receiving texts, and smashing spiders.

It was like they were slow-walking her into their horror movie, one piece of surrendered technology at a time.

"I did." Her editor sounded unsettled, like something about the material had disturbed him. "Esther, are you sure you want to go through with this? The drugs—"

"Are all cleared for use in this process. It's no more dangerous than dental sedation."

"People die during dental sedation."

"Then it's *less* dangerous than dental sedation. No one has died during one of Dr. Webb's 'procedures.'" Esther rifled through the release forms on her temporary desk, giving them one last quick review. "One man did have a stroke, but he had filled out medical disclosure forms ahead of time indicating that he had a pre-existing condition. He accepted the risks."

(And hadn't that just burned? She'd called his doctor, hoping to find a little underhanded manipulation of events, something that would point to a secret graveyard of buried secrets clawing at their coffins, yearning to break free. Instead, she'd found a doctor who was glad, if regretful, to confirm that his patient had undertaken the procedure against medical advice—and that he had been happy to sign off on it, although he had refused to tell Esther why his now-deceased client had been seeking Dr. Webb's services. Some stories wanted to stay buried.)

"Dammit, Esther, I—"

"Sent me here knowing that Webb was going to give the hard sell, and that I was going to crumble, because you have my psych evaluation from before I left on this assignment."

Silence from the phone. That was answer enough, really, and the only one she'd been expecting.

"You knew I wasn't going to be able to resist seeing her system from the inside. It's just one more form of repressed memory therapy, which means it's bullshit, which means I need to understand it well enough to tear it down."

"You promised to be objective."

"You sent me for a full observer's report on their program and methodology, to go along with Sunnie's report on the tech they've been willing to share. You knew what you were doing." He'd known she was a scorpion since the day he'd picked her up, young and hungry and toiling in the click-bait gossip blogs, turning out article after article in the hopes of that one big break that would change the world.

When the big break had come, it hadn't changed the world. It hadn't even changed her address. All it had changed was the type-face on her byline—and the place her articles appeared. Now she was print as well as electronic, a hyper-evolved modern journalist diving back into the den of the dinosaurs, trying to drag them kicking and screaming out of the path of the oncoming comet. So many of them seemed content to sit in their corners and die quietly.

Esther wasn't having any of that. The future was coming. The future was here. The future was not evenly distributed, and was never going to be, but people could at least keep writing about it, could keep pointing to its flaws and bellowing for the world to turn and open up its eyes. She had as much of an agenda as anyone else she knew. She simply thought, in the usual mammalian way, that her agenda was the right one. Her ideas were pure, and would protect people from those who would exploit them. All they had to do was let her show them.

"Promise me you're being careful."

"I've read all the documentation. I've spoken to my doctor."

"Have you spoken to your psychiatrist?"

This time, the silence was on her end, offended as much as stumped. On the other end of the phone, her editor sighed.

"When you took this assignment, you agreed to acknowledge that what had happened to your father would be a factor, and to remain in constant contact with your psychiatrist. That was our deal."

"Deals can change."

"Esther—"

"The window for gaining access to one of Dr. Webb's therapy pods is narrow. They're set up to run three scenarios at a time, for up to six patients." They were planning to expand, of course;

that was part of why the historically press-shy doctor had agreed to the article. The Institute hoped to expand their pod system, keeping the current dual system while also adding multiple "family size" pods, allowing them to enroll up to eight people in the same scenario.

("It will help people who've experienced a shared traumatic experience to move past it," Dr. Webb had explained, smiling coolly for the camera, looking like butter wouldn't melt in her mouth. Esther would have given a great deal for the name of her public relations coach. No one was this effortless on film without someone teaching them how. "Plane crashes, acts of terrorism, even more regrettably common incidents, such as abuse by a trusted coach or teacher, we'll be able to guide the people who come to us past that terrible reality and into a fiction that might teach them how to forgive themselves. How to forgive the world.")

Without a partner going under with her, Esther would be effectively locking up a two-person pod system for between six and sixteen hours, depending on the complexity of her scenario and how she chose to interface with it. During that time, the Institute would be limited in the number of patients they could see. It was hard not to feel smug about how she had effectively cut their available systems by one-third, all without doing anything beyond promising them a little press.

"I'm still not fully comfortable with this."

"Are you going to tell me not to do it? Or is this exactly what you hoped I'd do?"

Again, her editor sighed. "Just…please be careful."

"How much danger can I really be in?" Esther put the paperwork down. "It's not like the horror movie will be real."

FINAL GIRLS

"WHILE IT'S happening, the scenario will feel completely real," said Dr. Webb. She wasn't behind her desk anymore, or operating a bank of complicated controls: she was sitting on the edge of the table supporting the unused pod, hands folded between her knees, attention fixed on Esther. "If you eat, you'll feel full. If you drink, you'll feel hydrated. We'll be tending to your body's needs throughout the process, if it goes long enough. We've found that there's surprisingly little correlation between hunger felt inside the scenario and hunger felt outside the scenario."

"Meaning someone could starve to death in one of these things?" asked Esther.

"Meaning they're not intended for recreational use," said Dr. Webb firmly. "Our VR technology is and will remain proprietary. We can't prevent people from making the same breakthroughs we did, but we can at least slow down the process."

"I see," said Esther. "You know, progress is historically difficult to slow or stop."

"I'm a scientist," said Dr. Webb, with a flicker of humor. "I'm fully aware of the hubris inherent in saying 'oh, we're just going to keep this to ourselves.' But that doesn't mean I need to hand out my blueprints like candy. Someone was always going to develop fully immersive VR, whether for therapeutic purposes or because they really, really wanted to enjoy their favorite video games. Honestly, I was betting on porn driving this particular scientific advancement. No one is more surprised than me that my little research center was able to beat them to the post. We're getting away from the point. No one will be starving to death in one of my pods, because no one will be using them without medical supervision. A technician is assigned to monitoring both the vital signs of the user and the stability of the scenario at all times."

"How detailed are these scenarios?"

"It depends on the needs of the user," said Dr. Webb. "In the case of Diana and Kim, whom you've met and who have consented to my discussing their treatment with you, we didn't need much detail at all. They had a clear problem which they wanted to have fixed, and we were able to create a basic narrative which they then embroidered upon. You..."

"I'm a tourist," said Esther.

Dr. Webb looked faintly uncomfortable. "You can't think of yourself that way. No one is a tourist once the scenario begins. Whether you intend it or not, you're going to receive the full therapeutic experience. We're not set up for anything less."

"I don't have anything to fix," said Esther. She yawned. "Damn. Those pills work fast."

"They have to, if they're going to be effective," said Dr. Webb. "And everyone has something to fix."

Esther opened her mouth to say something else. The words turned into another yawn, and by the time it was over, her eyes were closed. She sank slowly down into the body of the pod, curled like a kitten, chest rising and falling in a steady, even rhythm.

Dr. Webb stood, all trace of geniality and concern bleeding out of her face as she looked down at the sleeping Esther. An onlooker would have been easily forgiven for finding something foreboding in her posture, which was more that of an undertaker than that of a doctor.

When she turned, her head technician was waiting behind her, backlit by the bright halogen glow through the open hallway door. She smiled at him, thin as a razorblade. He smiled back. His teeth were very bright.

"She's ready," she said.

"Yes, Dr. Webb," he replied, and reached for the waiting cart, loaded with syringes and bags of pharmaceutical solutions that would work their own strange magic on the sleeping woman.

It was time for the adventure to begin.

THERE WAS no sensation of falling, of fading from one reality into another: Esther closed her eyes on one world and opened them on another. There was a faint, nagging sense at the back of her mind that something was wrong. It faded, replaced by the sense that she had moved from one tense into another, that everything around her was—is—happening with a reality, an urgency, that she has never felt before.

She is standing in the living room of an empty house, floral wallpaper and exposed ceiling beams and carnival glass windows greeting her in every direction. She puts a hand against her sternum to still the pounding of her too-anxious heart, and the curve of her breasts has been reduced from a sentence to an epigram, barely present. She is thirteen years old, in the summer before puberty will hit her (did hit her? Might hit her? Present and future and past are tangled together like eels in a bucket, impossible to pick apart) like a freight train. Right now, she is still more child than woman, for all that she is technically a teen.

That her own age should be a revelation is less confusing to her than the scene around her. The house is older than any other house Esther has ever seen, except for maybe on television, where it seems like every house is an old one, like nothing has been built in the world since her grandparents were young. That's something else this house has in common with the ones she's seen on TV: her grandparents used to live here, before they died (passed away) and left the property to her—

To her—

"Esther, what are you doing? You're supposed to be carrying those boxes up the stairs!"

Her heart hammers even harder in her chest as she turns, and there he is, *there he is*, her father standing in the doorway, a stern expression on his beloved, bearded face. She runs to him before taking the time to think about the action, flinging her arms around his waist and burying her face in his shirt. He smells like cedar chips and sweat and leather, the scents she will always associate with him, until the day she dies.

(In a small, closed pod, miles and years and realities from this moment that never existed, the woman Esther would grow up to become bit down on her mouth guard, back arching away from the foam surface beneath her, every muscle in her body protesting this monumental lie. On the other side of a glass window, a technician in a long white coat frowned and adjusted the doses on her medication, sedating her until she subsided, relaxing back into the illusion of a home that never was, a moment that never happened, back into the *now*.)

"Esther, what's wrong? You're shivering." Benjamin Hoffman lets his daughter go and takes a step back, looking at her carefully. "Is it too cold? Do you need me to turn up the heat?"

Esther doesn't know why she's shivering—didn't even realize she was until he said something. She shakes her head, and answers, "No, Daddy. I guess I'm just a little overwhelmed with...

everything." She waves her hands, encompassing the house, the two of them, even the town outside.

"Ah." Benjamin never expected to be a father: thought that blessing was reserved for someone else, someone better and wiser and *luckier* than him. Now that he has his little girl, he's going to do as well by her as he can. He made that promise the day she was born. He's never broken it. "You know, peach, if you need to go stay with your Aunt Shira..."

"I don't want to stay with Aunt Shira," says Esther firmly. "I want to stay with you. I promised Mom I wouldn't let you be alone. She said you wallow."

Benjamin grimaces. "I suppose that's true," he says, in the careful, fragile tone of a man who is still adjusting to the idea of being a widower: still coming to terms with the existence of a world where his wife is not waiting in the next room, ready and even eager to step in and make the business of parenting a little easier to bear. He has so much to learn. He has so much motivation.

Esther's face is turned toward his, the light that slants through the carnival glass windows painting her skin in pinks and greens, and it doesn't matter that he's a simulation drawn from her own memories of her father: he loves her so much he could fill the world with loving. She has never been more beautiful, and he has never needed her more.

Benjamin Hoffman, dead for nearly twenty years, resurrected by a computer program that had barely been conceived of when he was still among the living, takes that girl in his arms, and holds her like he never, never wants to let her go.

"AND SHE'S under," said the technician, sounding profoundly satisfied with himself. He leaned back in his chair, cracking his knuckles theatrically, like a conductor getting ready to start his finest symphony. "Dr. Webb?"

"Esther Hoffman, age thirty-four," said Dr. Webb. Her tone was distant, almost clinical. It sounded like she was reading from a file, despite her empty hands. "Her father, Benjamin Hoffman, was convicted of child abuse and kidnapping when she was fifteen, leaving her in the custody of her maternal aunt. All charges were later dropped and his conviction overturned when it was discovered that his accusers had been guided by an unethical psychologist helping them to recover 'buried' memories. Unfortunately for Mr. Hoffman, vindication came too late: he had died in prison the previous year. Esther never forgave the system for failing her father, or the psychologist who'd effectively painted the target on his back, marking him as a stranger and a danger to the people of their new hometown."

"Her mother died, correct?" The technician pulled up a file, opening it to display various pictures of diaphanous ghosts. Many of them were modeled after deep sea jellyfish, strange and alien and organic. "Do we want to haunt her?"

"Esther has surprisingly few issues connected to her mother," said Dr. Webb. "Eliza Hoffman's death was not unexpected, and while it was, of course, a tragedy for their family, they had time to prepare. She didn't die suddenly. She made her peace with her daughter before she went. Nothing in Esther Hoffman's psych profile indicates a need for closure with her mother."

"She immediately actualized her father into the scenario. Perhaps—"

"She misses him. Not uncommon." Entirely understandable, in fact. Not even Dr. Webb could read something in need of fixing into the scene playing out on their view screen.

(She wondered, sometimes, whether anyone really understood that the true technical advance here—the thing that would put her institute in the history books, regardless of whether her admittedly time-intensive and potentially dangerous form of rehabilitation caught on—was the view screen. When her technicians watched a therapy session, guiding it from their keyboards, interjecting the beats and elements she instructed them to, they were watching *dreams*. They were guiding *dreams*. The interpretation and examination of dreams had gripped the human imagination for millennia and now, thanks to her, they could actually be touched, filmed, reviewed at leisure in the waking world. It was a game changer, and it was entirely hers. No one, ever, was going to take that away.)

The technician turned fully in his seat, frowning. She couldn't remember his name—she almost never remembered their names; they were interchangeable, true believers all, who came to her looking to change the world, never understanding that when the world actually changed, when she actually *did* it, hers would be the only name on the magazine cover. Or maybe they did understand, and they simply didn't care. Some people wanted change for the sake of change, and not for the potential fame it brought along for the ride.

"What are we going to do, then?" he asked. "We have to show her something. A little home movie of her father isn't going to cut it."

Dr. Webb tilted her head to the side, looking thoughtfully at the screen. "There's something we could try," she said, in a slow, deliberate tone. "How do you feel about managing a double session?"

The technician smiled.

STARTING A new school is always terrifying. Esther can't imagine a situation where it wouldn't be. She's done it before, twice, but both times, she still had a living mother; she wasn't the new girl with the dead mom, the girl everyone was primed to feel sorry for and judge. What if she doesn't seem sad enough? What if she seems *too* sad, and it tips her over into weird? She doesn't want to be the weird girl. There's too much responsibility in the role. The weird girl carries the weight of the world, and it isn't anything she's ever wanted.

She stands outside the middle school that will be her home for the next year, teaching her lessons she can't even conceive yet, and wonders whether she's going to throw up in the bushes before she can get up the nerve to walk toward the door. She'll definitely be the weird girl then. She's pretty sure throwing up on the school grounds gets you an automatic pass to Weirdoville, do not pass "go," do not get an invitation to the popular table.

Not that she wants an invitation to the popular table. There's too much responsibility there, too. She wants to be left alone. She wants time to mourn, and time to figure out who she is, in a world that doesn't have her mother in it. She's never been half an orphan before. It still fits her oddly, like a pair of jeans she'll have to grow into.

There should be a word. A word that means "daughter without a mother." Her father is still alive. She can't call herself an orphan.

But moments like this, she feels like one, and she doesn't know how to make it stop. She doesn't know if it *can* stop.

"They hold the classes inside the building, you know. I mean, that's what I've heard, anyway."

Esther flinches before she turns. "Huh?" she says, words gone, chased away by anxiety.

The girl behind her smiles a little, looking oddly understanding. "Hi," she says. "You must be the new girl. I'm Jennifer."

"You already knew there was going to be a new girl?"

Jennifer shrugs. "You moved into the house next to mine. I sort of followed you down the street. You never looked behind yourself."

It's a believable story—Esther knows she never looked back. Her nerve would have broken, and she would have run all the way home to lock herself in her bedroom and cry until the shaking stopped. Cathartic, maybe. Not a good way to avoid a visit from the truant officer.

Jennifer is still looking at Esther, and so Esther looks at Jennifer. The other girl is an inch or so shorter, round in the middle, with a tangle of blonde curls that frizz at the ends, seemingly less styled than vaguely tended, like weeds growing in an uncut yard. Her eyes are bright, and she's smiling. That's the nicest thing about her. It's been a while since anyone looked at Esther like she was something worth smiling at.

"I'm Esther," says Esther.

"Cool," says Jennifer. Then: "You want someone to show you to class?"

Esther very much does.

They have nearly identical schedules: Esther is in band while Jennifer is in her computer elective, learning about the language of bits and bytes and how to control some sort of virtual turtle. (It doesn't make any sense to Esther, but Jennifer just laughs when she says that, and says it doesn't matter; even though computers are the future, the future's going to need a soundtrack). The rest of the day they spend together, packed into the same small, boxy rooms, surrounded by their curious, faceless peers. Not *literally* faceless—that would be terrifying—but oddly uniform, blending into the background, until it seems like the world has been reduced to Esther and Jennifer, moving in their own private beams of light, standing out in stark relief against the rest of the colorless world.

Esther might be worried about how quickly she's latched onto this virtual stranger, if she weren't so wrapped up in her relief. She hadn't been sure she remembered how to make friends; had been afraid, really, that she'd lost the knack. It was always so *easy* back home, when the only weird thing about her had been "Esther Hoffman doesn't celebrate Christmas." Now she's Esther with the dead mom, Esther with the sad dad, Esther from out of town who doesn't know anything or anybody. She may not be a weirdo, but she walks in a cloud of weirdness, and Jennifer is saving her just by standing close without running away.

Everyone else can come later. She can make more friends, forge more bonds, once she's proven that she's good enough for this one.

All her classes are basically the same. She introduces herself to the teacher, who knew that she'd be joining them before she got there; she finds a seat; she is introduced as a new student, sometimes casually, sometimes with a mandatory "tell us something about yourself" that draws giggles from her new classmates. Esther doesn't begrudge them their amusement. She's been on the other side of the laughter, when someone new came to her old school. She knows there's nothing mean behind it, even as her cheeks burn red and her knees go wobbly.

(And isn't that knowing, that understanding of relief and self-consciousness and better-you-than-me, isn't it all too adult for her? Shouldn't she be crying in a bathroom somewhere, scared witless by this echoing new building with its rules she doesn't know, its casual traditions she may not have time to learn before graduation sends her to a high school all these kids have grown up anticipating, and which she has never seen? Middle school feeds into high school, yes, always has, but she should have had three years to navigate it, not a slightly slimmer slice of one. She should be so much more upset than she is.)

(In the real world, the technician frowned and adjusted her emotional response triggers, trying to nudge Esther closer to the child she appeared to be. It was impossible to take an adult fully back to the careless short-term thoughts of a pre-teen—impossible for now, anyway; they were getting closer all the time—but he could change her dosages, could adjust her perceptions, until she was thinking almost like her thirteen-year-old self. He had done it before, and he would do it again, over and over, until everything was understood.)

At the end of the school day, facts and faces chasing each other around her head like ponies on a racetrack, Esther follows Jennifer to the school doors and looks at her shyly, waiting to learn what the other girl is planning to do. To her delight and relief, Jennifer grins.

"Want me to walk you home?" she asks.

"*Yes*," says Esther, and Jennifer laughs, and the world is a little better.

THE ROUTE from the school to their neighborhood is a game of choose your own adventure, streets branching and twisting in all directions. Esther took the easiest route this morning, walking fast and not looking back. According to Jennifer, that isn't just the boring route, it's one of the slower ones—too many streetlights and crosswalks slowing the average speed of transit. Esther isn't sure why running into traffic is so appealing, but it is. It really, truly is.

The route Jennifer selects is winding, overcast with skeletal branches and coated in a thick layer of fallen leaves. She kicks them as they walk, her attention half on their surroundings, half on Esther.

"Where did you live before?" she asks.

Esther squirms inside her skin, feeling like she has come disconnected from everything around her. "California," she said. "We lived in California." The other side of the country; the other side of the *world*. Massachusetts has trees, but they're wrong, more like bushes with delusions of grandeur than the comfortable, towering eucalyptus of her homeland. These are trees that show their bones. She doesn't trust them. She would be a fool to trust them.

The leaves crunch underfoot, filling the air with a dry, unfamiliar scent. It's organic and sour but not unpleasant, and watching Jennifer kick flurries of leaves into the air, sending them falling like confetti, Esther can understand how people who were born here could love it. She's not sure she ever will. She's not sure she wants to. It would feel like a betrayal of her home, and of the mother who waits there for her to return, sleeping silent beneath the loam.

(The adult Esther never did return: went to college on the East Coast, learned to love the idea of seasons, of trees that lost their leaves, of new beginnings. She learned to live in an unhaunted world, one where the ghosts of her parents were only shadows seen out of the corner of her eye, and not memories trapped on every street corner, indestructible and unforgettable. In her pod, she twitched a little in her sleep, and was still.)

"Hey." Jennifer tugs her sleeve, pointing with her other hand. Esther follows the angle of her arm, the direction of her finger, and finds herself looking at a graveyard.

It is an old-fashioned thing, older and wilder and somehow more terrible than the graveyards of California, which are mossy and overgrown, but lack the weight of centuries. *There are more dead people in that ground than there are living people on this street*, thinks Esther, and shudders, unable to shake the feeling that something has gone utterly, catastrophically wrong.

"See?" says Jennifer, oblivious to Esther's discomfort. She's still smiling. She's standing on the edge of a sea of dead people, and she's still smiling. "That green one is mine."

It takes Esther a moment to realize that Jennifer is talking about a house on the other side of the cemetery, and not an especially mossy tombstone. "Oh," she says.

"Come on!" Jennifer steps off the sidewalk, sliding on the sides of her feet down the short incline to the cemetery fence.

Esther freezes, girl made of stone, as she watches her new friend squirm through a gap in the wall meant to separate the living from the dead. She has a choice here. She knows that. She can turn around, walk back to the school, and start the trip home anew, following a path she's already walked, safe and secure and free from any adventure. Also free from the risk of making a friend. Jennifer will see her as a chicken if she runs, and Jennifer won't be wrong.

Or she can slide down the side of the hill—can already almost feel the dirt moving under her feet, the familiar shift in the soil, carrying her onward, toward the consequences of her choices—and let Jennifer lead the way. She has the feeling that if she does that, Jennifer will be leading the way for a long, long time. Maybe for their entire lives.

She doesn't think she'd really mind. She's so tired of walking alone.

Esther slides down the side of the hill and follows Jennifer through the fence, into the graveyard where she waits. Jennifer smiles as she approaches.

"What took you so long?" she asks, and that's that: the compact is sealed. The story is begun.

___ 3. Chasing.

BACK IN the real world, the man at the controls to the scenario smiled to himself, watching the vital signs of the two women rise and fall in quiet harmony. They've been under for less than two hours—in Dr. Webb's case, less than one hour—and already, they're starting to synchronize. By the time they finish facing the challenges he has to set for them, they'll be old friends, thick as thieves and utterly loyal to each other.

The lights flickered. He barely noticed.

(Dr. Webb designed the system. She understood better than anyone that it was impossible to use without experiencing at least a portion of its power. No matter how hard he attempted to steer the psychological conditioning away from her, she would wake with a newly-formed lifelong friendship to the Hoffman woman boiling along her neural pathways. It would fade to a more subdued level if they didn't elect to go back under, which seemed likely, all things considered: Esther Hoffman was opposed enough to everything they did that she was unlikely to consent to multiple treatments. But nothing, no amount of time or distance, would erase it. They would always care about each other. That could be used.)

A muffled footstep from behind him caught his attention. Not quite enough to take his eyes away from the screen, where the two girls (so odd, to see them reimagined so young) were walking hand-in-hand through the virtual graveyard. It was a small scare, binding them together before the larger frights that were to come. They had been regressed to one of the safer ages, subject to neither the terrible elasticity of early childhood, nor the hormonal rages of their true teenage years. Changes made in the here and now would only revise, not rewrite completely.

"Did you get the burritos?" he asked. "I'm starving."

There was a rustle. He started to turn. The knife through his throat stopped him cold, pinning him back against the expensive leather of the chair. Eyes rolling, he scanned the darkness for his assailant, but found nothing. His hands rose, clawing at the hilt protruding from his flesh. They found no purchase against hardwood liberally smeared with blood, more of which was escaping all the time.

Eventually, his hands dropped away from the knife. The twitching continued for several seconds, until that, too, passed. His assailant waited until the stillness became absolute before stepping calmly forward and jerking the knife out of his throat, freeing one last hot gush of blood before it all faded to a trickle. From there, it was a simple matter to roll the chair into the corner and replace it with a fresh one, unburdened by inconvenient corpses.

Calmly, humming quietly, the new conductor of the bloody symphony reached for the keyboard and began to type.

WHEN ESTHER looks back on the last few years, it's like seeing her life reflected in a funhouse mirror. She knows everything happened, can still see herself there when she closes her eyes and concentrates, but sometimes it seems impossible that her world has been reshaped so completely and conclusively in just three short years.

The smell of the Massachusetts sky is familiar now, as familiar as the California coast's blend of eucalyptus, evergreen, and sea brine used to be. She walks in a world of fallen leaves and apple trees, of petrichor and old brick, and she is happy here, so happy that she can't imagine ever wanting to go back to where she came from. She no longer sleeps in the hall outside her father's door, driven by a fear she could never quite put a name to, one that whispered of his life cradled in her hands, preserved only by her stubborn refusal to ever let it go.

And there is Jennifer.

Rude Jennifer, loud Jennifer, brilliant Jennifer, fighting against a sea of people who say little girls shouldn't do math, or program computers, or dream of lab coats and white walls and the magical, infinite unknown. Weeping Jennifer, shattered Jennifer, unsure Jennifer, slipping her hand into Esther's after one body-blow too many to her ego, which is reassuringly human, despite the fact that Jennifer herself sometimes seems like a force of nature, a hurricane destined to destroy the Eastern seaboard, mistakenly pressed into the body of a human child. Jennifer who matches aggression with aggression, refusing to be bullied, refusing to back down, and there, always in her shadow and happy to remain there is Esther, best friend and confidant, who will one day be the power behind the throne she knows in her heart Jennifer will inevitably claim.

Esther, who excels in creative writing and journalism, but had to drop drama midway through her first semester when the stage fright paralyzed her in front of her classmates. Esther, who is no longer the new girl—who left that new girl behind long ago, the moment she chose to follow her friend into the aisles of the dead rather than walking on alone. Esther, sixteen years old and confused about almost everything in the world, from who she's attracted to all the way down to what she wants to be when the last bell rings at the end of senior year, but who knows two things for certain: she loves her father, and she and Jennifer are going to be friends for the rest of their lives. Let the world throw whatever it likes at them. She'll be holding onto Jennifer's hand, anchoring her to the ground while she builds her beautiful castles in the air.

"Esther, earth to Esther, can you hear me? Do you read?"

Esther shakes off the cobwebs that have gathered over her thoughts, turning to smile at her best friend. For a moment, it seems like Jennifer is doubled, the thirteen-year-old she met when she first moved to town sketched over the sixteen-year-old that Jennifer has become. The moment passes.

Jennifer: still short, still round, but now with the added benefit of breasts and hips, both of which grew in with staggering aggression during the summer of their fourteenth year. Esther would envy them, if not for the fact that they'd seem entirely out of proportion on her own longer, slimmer frame. They are both built exactly as biology wants them to be, complete, perfect organisms, designed to ensure their own best shots at survival. Jennifer's hair is still curly, still frizzy, but the blonde is shot through with panels of green and purple, painstakingly dyed in the upstairs bathroom of Esther's home. She wears jeans and a *Buckaroo Banzai* T-shirt, and everything about her is perfect.

Esther is sometimes less sure about her own perfection, despite Jennifer's insistent reminders that for one of them to be perfect, they would both have to be. She is taller, towering over Jennifer by almost a foot—towering even over many of the boys, who look through her like she isn't anything worth seeing. Her hair is dark and dense and the red panels Jennifer so carefully bleached and dyed for her are lost among the shadows of it all. She rather likes that, if she's being honest. She likes knowing that she's enough to overwhelm cosmetic changes. Unlike Jennifer, she is not, has never been, dressed to be seen; is as close to bland as she can get without a uniform to save her from choosing between types of denim, between shades of gray.

Jennifer should have abandoned her years ago. There are always eager young scientists in training ready to play Igor to the right upperclassman Dr. Frankenstein. But Jennifer has stayed, and Esther has stayed, and as long as they can both keep doing precisely that, there is nothing they cannot do.

"Sorry," says Esther, and shakes her head again. "I don't know what came over me."

"If we're going to stand here and talk about what's wrong with you, we're going to miss homeroom," says Jennifer, with the casual, artificial cruelty of the best friend, and Esther laughs, and on they walk, toward the future, toward the school.

All around them, the world is sketched in the colors of Halloween, just as it was on the day they first met—but if everything was strange and gray and unfamiliar on that long-gone, half-forgotten day, everything is color and light and comfort now. Esther knows every scrap of it, even as she knows that volunteers are already hard at work decking out the town square in orange silk streamers and bat-shaped lanterns.

(No crepe paper here, no. That was good enough for California, where it almost never rained hard before the end of October, but here, the decorations, and the people, must be made of sturdier stuff if they're going to survive the weather. She likes that about Massachusetts. The things here seem real in a way that things at home never did. It's odd, how a change of location can change the world so dramatically, but who is she to deny the evidence of her eyes?)

They step through the front doors and into hallways filled with cheerful monsters. Teens seem to hold to Halloween longer here than they did on the West Coast—or maybe that's a trick of the light, her memories of her old home growing fainter and more suspect with every passing day. Maybe the high schools were always a costume shop given social structure and permission to walk in the world for the entire month of October, and she had simply been too far away from them to ever know for sure. Now...

Now a ghost with pom-poms and pigtails flirts with a werewolf in a letter jacket, her lips painted cyanotic blue, his hands adorned with patches of fake fur that look more teddy bear than terror. Now a zombie runs down the hall, arms filled with books, the shambling speed of the undead forgotten in his rush to get to class. Now there are creatures of the night everywhere she looks, and the clarity of their monstrosity is comforting. Humans can be monsters too. Esther knows that better than most. At least for the moment, they wear their fangs on the outside, and she can see them before they bite her.

Case in point: a tall, elegant vampire pushes herself away from her locker, every movement a poem, every gesture a psalm. She is beauty given flesh, and were it not for the sharp, bitter warning in her eyes, Esther suspects she might be halfway in love with this creature of the night before the moment had the chance to pass.

"What are *you* supposed to be, Webb?" sneers the vampire, and the illusion is broken, as the illusion always must be. This is no siren, no seductress from the other side of shadow. This is

Daphne from down the block, always the prettiest, always the most poised, always posed to throw the first stone. "A laundry basket with legs?"

"I'm a mad scientist," says Jennifer, no trace of rancor in her tone. Esther envies her more than anything for that, for the ability to stare down her enemies and never bat an eye. "We don't need lip gloss. We have jumper cables."

"Oh, and I guess *she*," Daphne gestures toward Esther, a life-time of scorn in the motion, "is your creation?"

"If I were that good, I'd already have enough money to buy and sell this town ten times over," says Jennifer, still unruffled. "She's my assistant. Right, Esther?"

"Yesssssssssss, mathter," lisps Esther, like something out of one of the old Vincent Price movies, and Jennifer laughs, and she laughs, and some of the other kids around them laugh, and Daphne is neither vampire nor mean girl queen: Daphne is just another thwarted monster, crawling back to her crypt and swearing her revenge.

The bell rings. The hall begins to empty. Jennifer looks to Esther, concern flickering through her bravado.

"You okay?" she asks.

"I am," says Esther, and for once, she isn't lying: for once, she is just fine.

Just fine.

THE BLOOD on the floor had dried to a sticky mess, but the smell lingered in the air, too thick to be cloying, too strong to be overlooked. The figure at the keyboard paused, fingers going still, to watch the two girls walk into a classroom and close the door. There was no class programmed into the scenario: if they were asked later, they would both swear they had been attending a session on a different subject, something drawn from their own memories, stripped clean of identifying details and turned into a sort of "rest period" for the program, allowing it to compile the next segment of the scenario. They were safe, for the next few minutes, trapped in academic worlds of their own making.

It was time.

The figure reached into a pocket and produced a sleek black rectangle that looked like a cross between a thumb drive and a wireless booster. It slotted seamlessly into a USB port at the side of the main console, and just like that, it was done: the final step of the plan had been completed. All it had taken was the death of three employees and one of Dr. Webb's clients, a woman named Angelica Mathers, who had been scheduled to come in for a consultation on her debilitating arachnophobia.

Angelica Mathers was no longer afraid of spiders. Her body, which might never be found, was covered in them.

The woman who'd stolen Angelica's place, slicing her way into the facility like the finely-honed scalpel that she was—first taking the security systems offline, then bypassing the cameras, and finally killing two of the guards, all in the interest of unfettered access—dipped her hand into her pocket again. This time she produced a phone, sleek and slim and breakable. She raised it to her ear and pressed a button on the side, opening a connection to the sole number stored in its circuits.

There was a click. There was a stretch of silence, tenuous and thin. Finally, there was a voice on the other end, rendered electronic and strange by a dozen layers of encryption: "Report."

"The infiltration is a success," she replied, her voice like hemlock and honey. "With an added bonus: your Dr. Webb is in the system."

There was another stretch of silence, this time the silence of shock rather than the silence of connection. Finally, the voice on the other end demanded, "What do you mean?"

"I mean she has a reporter here, doing a write-up on the system, and she went in to the scenario they created to impress the media." The woman sniffed. "Probably shouldn't have done that. She's right in front of me. The scenario modifications you've uploaded will wash hers out real soon now."

"Did you—"

"I set all active scenarios to teen parameters, exactly as I was told. I'm a professional." Now she sounded disgusted, like the very thought of going off-script was inexcusable. "I assume that, should I be successful, I will receive full payment for both jobs."

"You've done less labor than anticipated."

"I've adapted quickly and accurately to a changing situation. Penalizing me for that would, of course, be within your rights, but I am afraid I would need to inform my colleagues of the chance that this could happen again at any time."

Another pause. "You don't need to threaten me."

"No one has threatened anyone. You have implied, and accurately, that I could be paid less than the agreed-upon fee for acquiring this technology and eliminating its creator, and there was no threat there: you are well within your rights to pay me according to the letter, and not the spirit, of our contract. I am well within my rights, should you choose this alternative, to inform my colleagues of your business decisions." Suddenly, her voice had teeth in it. "I agreed to work for you. I agreed to preserve your privacy as regards the materials you have asked me to acquire and the tasks you have asked me to perform. I am still allowed to discuss what kind of man you are. I think you'll find that an NDA which stops my tongue completely is *far* more expensive than simply paying me for services rendered."

"Be reasonable."

"I could say the same to you, could I not, and with far more cause?" The woman brushed at a spot of blood which had somehow found its way onto the sleeve of her coat. "You're paying for my time. If I am interrupted because of your indecision, and unable to complete my primary mission, you will still pay me in full. Now. How shall I proceed?"

The pause this time was shorter, and when the voice spoke again, it was with conviction. "Destroy her."

The woman smiled. "Excellent," she said, and hung up the phone without another word. Her profession required a certain amount of negotiation, and a certain amount of civility. What it didn't require was actual politeness. Very few people hired their corporate spies or sometime assassins on the basis of how well they said "please" and "thank you." Hiring was a matter of how well someone could get the job done, and she could get the job done very, very well.

Very well indeed. Leaning forward, she began to type.

THE LAST bell rings and the school day is over, unleashing a plague of high schoolers on the unsuspecting October afternoon. Esther and Jennifer step out of their last class, squinting in the sudden brightness of the sun, filling their lungs with the crisp taste of autumn growing ripe and ready on its insubstantial vine.

This is where we should stop, thinks Esther, with a sudden, nonsensical fierceness, like the whole world exists only to support this thought. *This is where we should wake up. It doesn't get better than this. A prelude and a friendship and we're done.*

"You okay?"

Jennifer is looking at her oddly again, a mixture of amusement and concern in her eyes. Only Jennifer ever seems to notice the way Esther zones out, like she's getting instructions from another place. Then again, only Jennifer ever seems to notice half the things Esther does. Esther has matured from new girl into nobody in this place, not weird enough for the nerd herd, not smart enough for the geniuses, comfortably existing in the liminal space where all the social circles collide. She likes it where she is. Jennifer always knows where to find her, and that's enough.

"I'm fine," says Esther, smiling quick and sharp and utterly sincere. "You ready?"

"I was *born* ready," says Jennifer. She mimes putting on a pair of sunglasses, and Esther laughs, safe within the embrace of a joke that has grown as well-worn and comfortable as an old pair of shoes. They begin to walk through the legion of monsters toward the door, letting the crowd carry them along without really trying. High school is a monster in its own right, alive and breathing and eternally hungry, and they, the students, are the parasites crawling on its skin. As long as they never attract its attention—as long as they can keep their heads down and their hands in clear view, never posing a threat—they can ride out the rest of their time here and escape clean and free.

Esther can't wait. Whatever comes next, she knows it will include Jennifer, and she knows that they will never look back. Some of the other kids call them lesbians, or less flattering things, and she supposes she minds, because any word can be an insult if it's thrown hard enough from the window of a moving sneer. Her love for Jennifer isn't about sexual attraction. She isn't sure yet where her sexuality lies, exactly, but she knows that it isn't with Jennifer. Jennifer is her sister, and nothing will change that. Ever.

Next to her, Jennifer is enthusiastically describing some clever new bit of computer wizardry, some trick of invented language and rapid code that makes the electrons sit up and dance. This, too, is normal for them: all Esther has to do is nod occasionally and make the noises that let her friend know she's still listening. Jennifer organizes her thoughts by talking them through, and doesn't care whether Esther understands what she's saying. Esther has found that if she allows Jennifer her data-dumps, the rest of their time together is less lecture, more conversation. It's a price she's more than happy to pay for her best friend's peace of mind.

(Far away and very close, in a pod designed to keep its occupants safe and dreaming, Dr. Jennifer Webb stirred, eyes moving fast behind closed lids, subconsciously aware that something had changed: that she was not supposed to be dreaming herself as a teenager, impressionable and wild and so wrapped in the embrace of her own changing brain chemistry that she was, at times, more horror than human. She was supposed to be dreaming a safe and stable pre-adolescence, making little tweaks, not sweeping changes. Then the drugs surged back, and the awareness of her own plight was gone, replaced by the dream.)

They walk out of the school and down the street, heading for the now-familiar shortcut that will take them across the cemetery and into their own backyards. Jennifer is winding down. Esther is preparing to rejoin the conversation as an active participant when a shadow passes across their path, followed by a vampire queen.

Esther stops. Jennifer doesn't, at first, too wrapped up in her retelling to understand the danger that Daphne and her gang represent. Esther grabs her wrist, pulling her to a puzzled halt.

"Wha—" Jennifer blinks, finally seeing the situation. Her eyes narrow. "Oh. Hi, Daphne. Sorry, didn't see you there."

"Freak," sneers Daphne.

Jennifer shrugs. "I have a higher than average intelligence, so you're technically within the meaning of the word. Can we help you with something?"

Daphne is flanked by five other monsters, all as carefully designed as she is, intended to be admired by their victims before they deliver the killing blow. There are no other vampires—that would be an insult to their leader, and anyone who's managed to survive in Daphne's grasp for this long is smart enough not to insult her—but there are two ghosts, and a werewolf, and a creature from the Black Lagoon. The last of them is a witch, all candy-colored spangles and cartoony makeup. None of them should be particularly frightening. All in a group like this, they're terrifying.

Daphne's upper lip curls back as her sneer grows more pronounced. "We thought it was time we reminded you of where you stand at school."

No one ever says the name of the school, thinks Esther wildly, getting a little dizzy on the terror of the moment. They're outnumbered, and one of the ghosts is on the track team, while Jennifer is infamous for treating even the hundred yard dash as an excuse for a stroll. They'll never get away. *I don't even think I know the name of the school. Why does no one ever say the name of the school?*

"We're not at school right now," says Jennifer calmly. "I guess that means we're not standing anywhere."

Jennifer has never been able to resist the opportunity to talk back, has been in trouble for her attitude so many times that Esther has long since given up on trying to keep count and simply settles for keeping an eye on Jennifer, a vain attempt to keep her friend out of trouble. It doesn't work, but at least Esther feels like she's doing something.

Right now, Esther feels like she's watching a train wreck in slow motion. Daphne steps forward, and there isn't any chance for them to run. Not today. Not yesterday. Maybe not ever.

"You mouth off too much," says Daphne. "That mouth's going to get you hurt one of these days."

"Like today," jeers the witch. Her words seem to put some steel in Daphne's spine, and warn Jennifer that something bad is about to happen.

Jennifer steps back, away from the advancing Daphne. She reaches behind herself, and Esther grabs her arm, holding her tight. Both of them are terrified. Esther wonders if Jennifer's fear is the same as her own, hot and cold at the same time, laced with thick bands of shame. How is that they always wind up here? Why do they never run before there's no more time?

Next time I'll run, she thinks fiercely.

Then Daphne's fist is impacting with Jennifer's nose, sending the shorter girl sprawling off the sidewalk and down the shallow hill between them and the cemetery fence. Someone shoves Esther, sending her after Jennifer, falling fast enough that they're together when they slam into the fence. It's old and rusty, the chain links weathered and improperly maintained; they bite into her skin, scraping chunks of it away, leaving her bleeding. Jennifer makes a sound that is somewhere between a gasp and a moan. Esther looks over, eyes wide, terrified of what she'll find.

Jennifer hit the fence face-first. Blood is cascading from her nose, drenching her, making her look like the victim of some terrible attack...which, in a way, is exactly what she is. They're teenagers now, not children, and they should know better than to hurt each other like this.

Daphne is laughing. Esther turns to see her standing at the sidewalk's edge, flanked by her monstrous cronies, a wide smile on her face.

"Aw, did you slip and hurt yourselves?" asks Daphne, a taunting, jeering note in her voice. "Too bad, so sad. Be more careful next time, why don't you?"

"Fuck you!" shouts Esther. Daphne looks stunned. For a moment—one bright, beautiful moment—Esther feels triumphant and strong, like she's actually managed to fight back.

Then she sees the rage blossom in Daphne's face, and knows how badly she's messed up.

"Run!" shouts Jennifer, grabbing Esther's hand and dragging her toward the familiar gap in the fence, the one they know like the back of their hands, the one they've never seen Daphne or her friends squeezing through. Esther stumbles to her feet and lets Jennifer lead her, Jennifer who is running for once, motivated by danger as she could never be motivated by a P.E. teacher. The two of them squeeze through the gap, Esther widening it so Jennifer will be better able to fit, and they're running, they're running as hard and as fast as they can, all too aware of the pounding of feet behind them, of the high, bright laughter of people who have nothing to lose, not really, not like they do.

Jennifer trips on a tombstone, her hand yanked out of Esther's by the shock. Suddenly unmoored, Esther flies forward until her momentum is halted by an open grave. She tumbles into it, slamming hard into the dirt at the bottom, feeling the air knocked entirely out of her. Not just the air: her bladder was full when she slammed down, and the combination of fear and momentum has been enough to knock at least some of the urine out of her as well. She sprawls where she fell, struggling to breathe, fighting not to cry.

Somewhere behind her, she hears Jennifer squeal, a thin, pained sound, like a rusted door being forced open. Then, from above:

"Roll over, skank, or we'll hurt her."

Esther rolls onto her back, not caring if Daphne and her friends see that she's wet herself, or how terrified she is. She never expected them to escalate like this. Maybe *they* didn't expect it to escalate like this. Sometimes things get out of hand.

Daphne is standing at the edge of the grave, perfectly framed by the slim slice of sky that is all Esther has remaining to her. She smirks, and then she spits, striking Esther squarely in the face.

"See? The more you try to stand up for yourself, the further you have to fall," says Daphne, like a babysitter explaining to her charges why they have to go to bed even though they're not tired. She spits again. Her cronies follow suit, gathering around the edge of the grave and clearing their throats until Esther feels like she's caught in a warm, cruel rain.

Her father has said, more than once, that he's grateful she's a girl, because girls aren't cruel to one another the way boys are. She's known since long before her mother died that this was just wishful thinking, the sort of lie someone tells themself when they can't think of anything better to say. Cruelty has no gender. The expressions of it can be trained one way or another, but even that isn't innate: it's all in what people are told will be possible, and not at all in who they actually are.

FINAL GIRLS

The girls surrounding the grave (*her grave*) seem to be losing interest in the game. Daphne kicks one last clod of dirt down on her.

"Stay out of our way," she instructs, before turning and stalking toward the fence, taking her flunkies with her.

There is no sign of Jennifer, no sound. Esther sits up, pressing her back into the corner of the grave, and weeps like her heart is breaking.

Maybe it is.

___ 4. Closing.

THE DEAD man had stopped moving once he'd finished bleeding out. It was a bit of a pity, really. The technology in this place was fascinating, and she would have enjoyed having someone to discuss it with.

For every development coveted by her employers there were three or four more, intended only to support it, which were revolutionary in their own right. The woman picked at the spot of blood on her sleeve again, unable to take her eyes off the screen. She'd fed this scenario in, modifying the pieces that were already extant as it began escalating a tale of childhood bullies and friendly, vaguely-threatening spirits to something that would be far more entertaining. The exact shape wasn't her doing, or that of the man who'd hired her. That was the work of Jennifer Webb and Esther Hoffman, their minds acting in concert without any communication between them as they influenced the scenario's guidelines, making them plausible, even believable. And then, because this form of therapy was designed by people who wanted it to be *seen*, the situations they created were broadcast in clear, clean images on the screen, as available for viewing as any film.

She was watching dreams. She knew that, and it amazed her. After a lifetime spent schooling herself to be as unimpressed as possible, it was almost refreshing to spend a little time gaping like a yokel catching their first glimpse of a city.

The people who hired her wanted this technology for the reprogramming advances it offered: brainwashing, rather than therapy. Deviants could be remade into productive members of society. Criminals could be transformed into model citizens. Most of all, enemies of the state could be given a new place and a new purpose as spies for the people who paid for their good behavior. This would change everything, and Dr. Webb had been frittering it away on bed-wetters and people with daddy issues. Really, the surprise wasn't that she was sitting here, watching the destruction of a dream. The surprise was that it had taken this long.

When word got out about what had happened here, what was *about* to happen here, the destruction of minds and personalities in the crucible of a therapy session gone wrong, it would be the end of Dr. Webb's dream…and her reputation, both professional and personal. No one would raise a flag in a martyr's name for her, the Frankenstein who got what she deserved.

The woman settled deeper into her chair, wishing for popcorn, and smirked. This was going to be fun.

THE SUN has slipped below the horizon with incredible, almost malicious speed, leaving Esther to crawl her way out of the grave in the darkness, spit drying on her face and urine drying on her legs. She doesn't like horror movies—those are Jennifer's darlings, short, sharp, controlled bursts of fear to lighten up a dark night—but she feels like she's living in one now, like she's some unspeakable creature rising from the unhallowed ground.

"Jennifer?" she whispers, her voice a hiss, bouncing off the headstones, returning nothing.

Her mouth tastes like blood and the heels of her hands are skinned from her fall, leaving them easy prey for every piece of gravel and clot of dirt. Still, she keeps pulling herself forward. Nothing feels like it's broken. She could probably stand, if she had to. Could probably run, if she had to. She doesn't test either thought. It's easier, in the here and now, to crawl, no matter how painful it is. This is all she deserves.

Someone is crying, and somehow Esther finds it in herself to stand. Once she's on her feet, it's a simple thing to turn toward the sound. Without even thinking about it, she's running, quickly reaching the sort of speeds that her gym teachers have always known she's capable of.

Jennifer is huddled in the shadow of a crypt, her face almost unrecognizable under the mask of mud and blood and bruises. Esther drops to her knees, reaching for her friend, and Jennifer reaches back, and they cling to each other, both of them weeping. Once the tears come, it's difficult to make them stop. They escape in great, shuddering gasps, Jennifer clinging to Esther, Esther clinging to Jennifer, and it feels like the world must split open and swallow them whole. What else can there be left for them?

Not homework. Their backpacks are gone, lost in their headlong flight across the cemetery. Even if Esther thought they'd still be out there to be found, she wouldn't go looking. They were unattended for too long. Daphne and her gang had too many opportunities for mischief. They can't be trusted anymore.

Not curfews. She and Jennifer were supposed to be home hours ago, judging by the moon, by the absence of the sun. Her father will be scared, and as soon as he sees her, all that fear will transform into anger—first at her, and then at the bullies who created this situation. He'll go into a towering rage. Nothing she says will be able to stop him, and on some level, she knows she won't really try, that she'll want to see him rain down fire and brimstone on the people who hurt her. But it won't help. It won't change anything for the better. It may change things for the worse. Daphne and her gang have dealt a devastating blow to people they see as outside the social structure and hence out of their control. If Esther and Jennifer keep their heads down and keep out of the way, this could be where it ends.

But her father isn't going to let that happen. As soon as he knows, things will escalate.

She could hide it. The thought is a lightning bolt across the storm clouds of her mind, brightening and dispersing them for a single heartbeat. Yes, she has scratches. Yes, she'll have bruises. But no one hit her. Unlike Jennifer, she won't have a single injury she can't explain away with an easy and believable lie. She could walk away from this.

Jennifer can't. Jennifer's nose looks like it might be broken, and the skin around both her eyes is dark and puffy, already well on its way to swelling them shut. For her to get away without a lecture, she would have to leave her friend to face it alone.

(In a pod, in another world, another time, another tense, the adult body of Esther Hoffman frowned in discontent and sour memory. There had been a few situations like this in her real teen years—situations the scenario no doubt pillaged to make this one more believable. That Esther, the Esther with two dead parents and no close friends, had been more than happy to walk away, to save herself at the expense of everyone around her. That Esther still existed in her safe, secure pod…but she was dying a little more with every second that passed, and she was defenseless to save herself. Another Esther was taking her place. An Esther who made different choices.)

"Can you stand?" Esther asks, offering Jennifer her hands.

Jennifer sniffles. Even the sound is painful. Then she clears her throat and spits, and even in the darkness, it's clear that her spit is thick with blood. "They didn't break my legs," she says, and takes Esther's hands, pulling herself to her feet. They stand that way for several seconds, both of them wobbling, drawing strength and stability from each other even when they have nothing to spare for themselves.

"Did they hurt you?" Jennifer asks.

It's a complicated question. In the end, all Esther can do is nod, unable to really put the size of her pain into words. Jennifer nods in understanding. They slip their arms around each other, still holding each other up, and begin to walk—Esther shuffling, Jennifer limping, both of them broken—across the cemetery toward the waiting lights of their homes.

They have bled on this ground. They have wept on this ground. They have been bathed in spit and urine, and while those fluids might carry less reverence than blood or tears, they still have their uses. As they walk, the shadows gather thick and deep behind them, twining into terrible tangles that have no business here, in this suburban graveyard, under this previously innocuous autumn moon. The girls don't look back. They are focused on what's ahead, and unwilling to look at what's behind.

They don't see the dirt begin to throb, pulsing as steadily as an undying heart. They don't hear the creak of the hinges within the standing crypts, or see the moss on the headstones begin to blacken and die.

When the first bony hand thrusts upward from the ground, they are long gone, and that may be the only thing that saves them.

AS ESTHER expects, her father is livid. More than livid: her father is incandescent with rage, so infuriated that he would burn the whole town to ashes if he thought he could get away with it. She stands in the living room, muddy and weeping, as he grabs his coat from the rack and yanks it on.

"No more," he says. "Do you hear me, Esther? *No more.* These girls have made you miserable for long enough. I didn't intervene before, because you asked me not to, but this changes things. Do you understand me? I want you to say that you understand me."

Esther's answer is another cascade of tears, her right hand flexing, like she thinks she can summon Jennifer back to her side if she wishes hard enough. Jennifer is at home right now, being fussed over by her parents, having the blood wiped from her lips and the tears wiped from her cheeks. She's hurt worse, and so while her parents may be angrier in the end, they'll wait until they're sure that she's okay. She'll have a stay of execution. Esther almost envies her for that.

Only almost, because they'll be heading for the same chopping block once Daphne's parents get involved. The thought gives her the strength to speak. "Please, Daddy," she says. "I just want it to be over. Please, can't we let it be over?"

"These girls deserve to be punished for what they've done."

They do, they do, there's no question that they do. Esther wants to agree with him, to agree that it's time to rain down fire and brimstone, and yet... "They'll take it out on us when nobody's looking. You know they will."

"I didn't raise you to run away from a fight."

She wants to tell him that he did exactly that. That when he chose to run rather than stand and deal with the aftermath of her mother's death, he taught her that anything can be escaped, if you're just willing to run far enough. She doesn't. Instead, she swallows, and asks, "Can't we wait until morning? Then we can talk to Jennifer's parents. See what they want to do."

Her father stands and frowns at her for a long moment, taking in the redness of her eyes, the holes in the knees of her jeans. He wants to fight this. She can see it in every inch of him. He wants to ride out like a pillar of fire and burn everything that has dared to touch his daughter, his baby, his precious little girl. But he also wants her to love him as much as he loves her, and he is smart enough in the ways of parenthood to know that if he disregards her wishes in this matter, she will trust him a little less, come to him a little less often, and that the erosion of her childhood hero wor-ship—inevitable as it is—will progress a little further. He would rather be her hero than her savior.

"I don't like this," he says, but his voice is soft, some of the fire leeching out of it. She's won. It's a hollow victory, filled with terri-ble teeth and unkindnesses, but she's won it all the same.

"I know, Daddy," she says. She goes to him then, and he takes that girl, and he holds her, while outside the night grows deeper and darker and wilder all the time.

Next door, in a house that might as well be identical (might as well have been designed by the same props department, in fact, because why would they waste processor power on decorating the houses anything other than alike?), Jennifer is eating a bowl of vanilla ice cream, wincing every time the cold hits one of her back molars, which she's fairly sure has cracked. She's praying it hasn't really; that this is some strange new form of bruising that will pass by morning. If there's no damage severe enough to require medical intervention, she might be able to keep her head down and keep her parents from seeking retribution. Once the dentist gets involved, it's all over.

She wants Daphne and her friends to pay, of course. Has always wanted them to pay, ever since she was a chubby, gawky preschooler watching other people walk through the world with ease and grace, while she was still trying to find her own feet on a consistent basis. It wasn't just that they were pretty: Jennifer has given plenty of thought to the idea of prettiness, and has long since come to the conclusion that anyone can be pretty, if they're willing to spend the time, effort, and money. It's that they were willing to play every game for keeps, even back then, turning little social strategies into a step toward mutually assured destruction. Jennifer has better things to worry about, has always had better things to worry about. But still, they hurt her, and sometimes she wishes they understood what that felt like. Sometimes, in a small, guilty corner of her heart, she wishes someone would hurt *them*.

Had Esther and Jennifer been ordinary girls, living in an ordinary world, that might have been where things ended: with anger, and resentment, and a tooth that would need repair. With slinking back to school, tails between their legs, spirits dimmed, finally put into their places...at least until enough time had passed, at least until they started to remember who they were. It was a drama that had played out hundreds of times, all across the world, written in a thousand different languages and performed with a million different players. If there had been nothing special about them, the rest could not have happened.

But they were not, are not, ordinary girls. They are the regressed hearts and minds and experiences of two adult women, locked into a virtual recreation of their own teenage skins, living through a situation designed to stimulate an impossibly intense emotional response, intended to *break* them. The real Esther grew up an orphan, daughter of a murdered man, with skin as thick as a rhino's hide and hands that ached from going unheld. The real Jennifer grew up too smart and too stubborn and too sharp for her own good, with no one to hold her up, only to hold her back. They are better together, here, in this make-believe adolescence, than they ever were alone...but they are also not ordinary, and their wishes have consequences. Their story has no chains to hold it down.

In the cemetery, the ground roils like the skin of a roadkilled animal being devoured from within by a thousand tiny, mindlessly chewing mouths. Skeletal hands break the loam, pulling themselves upward, outward, being reborn into a night that is suddenly alive with a million tiny clicking, popping sounds as their bones snap back into their original positions. This is terrible. This would be terrible enough. But ah, "enough" has never been the goal of such terrors.

Thick liquid, brackish and smelling of the grave, oozes out of the earth around the feet of the risen dead. It pools there, bubbles forming on its surface, releasing more unspeakable odors every time they pop. Then, as slowly as it appeared, the liquid runs up the length of the long bones of their legs, sticking there, sloughing off its decay, becoming muscle and sinew and skin. Piece by piece, the dead are reassembled, until they look perfectly human once more. No: better than human. Their skins are without flaw, save for a certain pallor which unites them, regardless of race, in a grayish undertone. They look as if they have been locked indoors for a hundred years, a thousand, millennia of isolation away from the open air.

They look dead.

But their faces are fine; their hair is thick and lush and lustrous; their bodies are smooth and chiseled, ripe with muscle and lush with fat. They span the gamut of human experience, and all of them are naked, and all of them are dead. They turn blank eyes toward the lights at the back of the houses occupied by Esther and Jennifer and their families. Then, as if in answer to a tone that only they can hear, they turn, seamless as swallows, and begin to walk away from those two houses. They begin to walk toward the school.

Their feet make no sound on the soft earth. Very soon, there is nothing left to show that they were ever there at all.

THE BEAUTY of the horror movie is in its distance. The things that happen are happening on the other side of a screen, terrible but removed, unable to touch the viewer anywhere outside of dreams. In dreams, anything is possible. In dreams, the Blob can ooze up from a shower drain, the man with the knives on his hands can stalk a boiler room that never was, the Wolfman can howl outside a bedroom window. But still, there is always the knowledge that the television can be turned off, that the movie will end, that the sleeper will wake; there is the understanding, primal and instinctive, that all this too shall pass.

Esther removes her clothes, shuddering at the smell of urine, at the way the fabric peels away from her skin. She feels like she has survived a war. The feeling does not pass as she showers, sluicing away the mud and blood that cover her, or as she bandages her hands and knees. She crawls into bed still shuddering, somehow convinced that things are very, very wrong, that things will never be right again. She is more right than she knows.

Jennifer has already showered, already had her face washed like that of a much younger child, and crawled into her own bed when Esther's head hits the pillow. That is the cue. For the two of them to face the next part of the scenario together, they must fall asleep together; they must move from segment to segment together. It is the most artificial piece of an artificial world, this careful control of their movements, when normally they are allowed—expected, even—to choose their own path through the narrative. Esther closes her eyes and Jennifer is asleep, sitting up in bed with her notebook open on her knees. The pen falls from her hand to land on the carpet, uncapped, unable to dry out, because it is only set dressing, nothing real. Nothing of importance. It is only here to lend credence to the scene.

The girls sleep, and as they sleep, they see the risen dead marching on the small, nameless town where they have carved out a space for themselves and for their impossible friendship: they see them, pale and gray and naked, walking down sidewalks and along culverts, their eyes trained forward, toward some unknown and unknowable destination.

They see the moment when a college student stumbles from the bar where he's been drinking away his problems and nearly collides with a naked woman, beautiful as the sunset, her eyes locked on the horizon. They see him light up, sure that his night is taking a turn for the better.

"Hey, you look cold—" he begins, and then the woman's teeth are at his throat and her hands are at his belly, ripping with a strength that is inhuman and impossible, so impossible that for a moment his mind simply shuts down, refusing to acknowledge that this could be happening, and when the moment passes, it is followed by another moment, twice as terrible, in which all of this is real, is real, is so terribly, terribly real. His blood is between her teeth and on her hands and in her mouth, and he dies before he can find the strength to scream. The woman, the dead woman, takes what she wants from him and drops him to the sidewalk, licking her lips, which are redder now than they were before.

There is a new light in her eyes, and a new sureness in her step, as she turns to look toward the bar he emerged from. She sees. She *understands*. She beckons the nearby dead to walk with her to the door, and together, they lay silent siege. Not entirely silent: the screaming has time to start now, and time to continue, and time to die.

Their victims do not rise, but lay where they have fallen, dead, ripped open and exsanguinated, drained of everything that made them who they were. They are not a part of this narrative. They were barely a part of this story.

The dead continue to move.

THE SOUND of footsteps outside the viewing room caught the woman's attention before she was fully aware of it. She whipped around, eyes narrowing, and peered at the half-open door. Lab protocols called for viewing rooms to be unlocked whenever in use, to increase accountability and prevent later lawsuits. The question of patient privacy was irrelevant: while Dr. Webb was a licensed therapist, none of her technicians shared her qualifications, and all the patients were required to sign a dozen releases before they entered an active pod, agreeing to let their sessions be viewed and even recorded. Given how easy it would be—how easy it *was*—for an unethical operator to twist an ongoing scenario, the accountability was an absolute requirement.

She had known this when she had infiltrated the facility, and when she had killed the original operator to take his place. She had simply been hoping to be able to slip out without killing anyone else. It wasn't the loss of life that bothered her: she'd done much larger jobs than this one, some with fatalities that numbered in the double digits. It was the loss of potential income. She had been hired to get Dr. Webb's data, distort any active scenarios, and discredit her work at the same time, not to destroy the place. That would have cost her employer substantially more. It was vexing, thinking about the lost income.

Slowly, she slipped out of her chair and moved to one side, where she wouldn't be visible to anyone stepping into the doorway. Let them think the scenario had been left to run temporarily unattended: she'd read enough of their documentation to know this was allowed when things weren't at a particularly tense juncture. For things like the scene in the school hallway, which had been necessary mostly as a transition between the increase in the two girls' ages and the graveyard, she could have gone for a glass of water and no one would have thought twice about her absence.

But on the screen, the dead were walking, returning to the graveyard, moving toward the homes of the two girls who woke them, calling them from their eternal rest. Their skins were slick with blood, and their eyes were filled with the screams of the slaughtered, alive in a terrible bright way. On the screen, the light in Esther's room had just come on, followed shortly by the light in Jennifer's. This was not a casual moment. This room should not have been unattended.

"Hello?"

The voice was light, female, and low to the ground. The hidden woman relaxed slightly. She didn't care whether her targets were male, female, or agender: what she cared about was her ability to overwhelm them with a minimum of fuss. Small people went down faster. Small people were thus to be preferred.

There was a soft sound, as of someone stepping hesitantly forward. The woman melted further back into the shadows. The longer she could delay this confrontation, the more the odds would be on her side.

She could see her uninvited guest now, through the space created between the hinge of the open door and the doorframe. It was a petite woman in a white lab coat and a dark sweater, her hair pulled back into a loose ponytail that hung most of the way to her waist. She was pretty, in an abstract sort of way; it would be a shame to kill her.

The woman flexed her hands. Many things were a shame, and had to happen anyway, for the benefit of the job.

"Tyler?" said the invader, taking another step forward. "Tyler, where are—" Her foot hit the edge of the pool of thick, largely congealed blood. She stopped as she felt the texture of the floor change, and looked down, and went very still and very pale at the same time, until she could almost have passed for one of the dead things in Esther and Jennifer's shared scenario. Her eyes bulged in her head, only a little at first, but more and more as the pressure of her captive scream grew. Finally, she opened her mouth, preparing to set that scream free.

The woman moved, quick as a thought, grabbing the sides of the invader's head and twisting hard to the right. There was a brittle snapping sound, followed by the scent of the invader's bowels voiding themselves, and all tension went out of her, replaced by the limp, floppy heaviness of the dead. The woman let her go. She fell to the floor, landing with a splat in the congealed blood.

The woman sighed.

She could walk away now, leave the scenario to run to its natural conclusion, leave the remaining technicians to stumble across the bodies of their peers and mask her intrusion with their own panicked response. She would have to leave the drive behind, but it would upload once it finished copying the data, placing everything safely in the cloud, ready to be collected when she next had use of a secure terminal. In the case that a break-in could not be performed seamlessly, it was always better to make it large, aggressive, and eye-catching. That increased the chances of the break-in's true purpose being utterly obscured as the police swarmed over everything, ripping through haystacks in search of needles that had never been concealed. She could get away clean, if she left right now.

But she wouldn't be able to guarantee that Dr. Jennifer Webb would die in her self-inflicted horror movie. She wouldn't be able to look at her employer and remind him that when he asked for the best, he got her, making her bill less a contractual obligation and more a tithe to a well-inclined goddess of crime. If he had wanted someone who would walk away and leave the job half-finished, he would have gone with one of her peers, faceless, foolish creatures who put more stock in their skins than in their professional pride.

With another sigh, the woman bent and grasped the intruder's ankles, using them to drag her into the corner. It was dark enough, and the blood was thick enough, that the trail this created barely changed the timbre of the room. She still had time.

Calm—ever and always calm—the woman reclaimed her seat and began once more to type.

___ 5. Capture.

ESTHER WAKES with a gasp, what feels like the ghost of a scream clogging her throat and choking her so that she can't quite catch her breath. She bends forward, pressing a hand against her sternum, feeling the anxious, unwavering pounding of her heart. Whatever she dreamt, it has scared the life out of her.

It's that unease, that feeling that something is *wrong*, that drives her from her bed to the window. The cemetery is a black stain against the lights of the town, which twinkle, fairy-like, all around it. She's often glad that she didn't live here until she was old enough to understand that the cemetery wasn't *actually* a light-sucking monster lurking just outside her bedroom. She can't imagine how Jennifer grew up on the cemetery's edge without becoming even weirder than she already is.

But tonight, the cemetery seems to pulse, like something in it has been sparked back to life, waking and stretching and stirring upon the world. Tonight, the darkness is deeper and shallower at the same time, a contradiction she feels in her bones, that feels like it would be delighted to rip her stem from stern. The world is *wrong*.

A patch of light amongst the dark catches her eye. She turns, and for a moment, she would swear she sees a face looking up at her from beyond the fence, pale and silent and somehow inhuman. Then the moment passes, the face moves, and she is alone again.

Her phone vibrates, dancing on her nightstand. She grabs it, disconnecting it from the charger, and is unsurprised to see a text from Jennifer. Unsurprised, and oddly unsettled, because if she's getting texts, she's really awake. This strangeness, this twisted world, is not a dream.

U UP?

YES, she responds, and follows it with, SOMETHING WOKE ME. NOT SURE WHAT.

THERE'S SOMEONE IN THE BACKYARD, reads Jennifer's reply.

Esther is about to ask her who, what she saw, why it woke her, when a new sound is added to the world, and she loses her patience for such easy questions: a scream rises from the downstairs, so high and pained that for a moment, her brain refuses to acknowledge it as human. Surely it's a raccoon with its leg stuck in a trap, or a fox—she's heard foxes can scream, although she's never heard it with her own ears—protecting its territory near an open window. It can't be human. It *can't* be her father.

Then the scream breaks into a shuddering sob, deeper and broader and less possible to ignore, and Esther runs, still in her flannel pajamas, to the hall, down the stairs, into the living room, where three of the perfect, pale people have converged upon her father. He is bleeding from a great wound in his shoulder, raw and ragged and surprisingly blue inside, shimmering with all the colors she's glimpsed at the butcher counter in the grocery store, the ones that have no place inside of a person. Esther freezes in the living room door, mouth working soundlessly, body seeming to catch fire and turn to ice in the same instant. Everything is floaty and far away, dreamlike.

I'm dreaming, she thinks, and the thought is warming and cooling at the same time, like a mug of hot cocoa with a dish of vanilla ice cream: perfectly mundane, perfectly reasonable, perfectly safe. She is dreaming, and none of this is happening to her—

(—and far away, a woman who no longer quite knew who she was stirred and moaned in her chemically-induced sleep, fighting against the drugs that fought with equal fierceness to keep her under. She no longer appreciated the *wrongness* of the world she dreamed: only that she needed to run, to flee, to save Jennifer before the dark could take them both down.)

—and that means she'll wake up soon, safe and sound and untouched by any impossible horrors from the wrong side of the grave.

Her father's wildly rolling eyes find her face, fix on it, and widen slightly, focusing through the pain, which must be unbearable and immense. Esther can't wrap her mind around the scope of the pain her father is feeling, and so she pushes it aside in favor of taking a shaking step forward, licking her lips as she tries to force them to remember how speech is made.

"Esther," whispers her father. His voice is cracked and shattered from the screaming, and she knows, she *knows* that these are the last words he'll ever speak to her. These are the words she'll preserve in the bell jar of her heart for the rest of her life, using them to shape and define herself long after the actual sound of his voice has faded into unmemorability.

"Esther," he whispers again, and doesn't scream, not even when one of the terrible *things* rips a chunk out of his bicep with its teeth. They look so close to human, but they're not. Even their clothes are wrong, ill-fitting and torn in places, seemingly stolen from their original owners. People who didn't need them anymore. "Baby girl, *run*."

The last word becomes a wail, and one of the things—a woman by shape, with eyes like ice—turns toward the door where Esther stands. There is blood smeared all across the bottom half of her face, thick and gory, lipstick that will never catch favor with the fashion elite.

"Esther," she purrs. Her voice holds all the life her eyes do not. "Why, what a pleasure it is to meet you. I suppose I owe you thanks. You're the reason that I'm here. The reason that we're all here."

(The dead woman had an assassin's face, and as the assassin herself sat behind the terminal which controlled Esther's private nightmare, she smiled. Oh, this was going to be delicious. This could never have been anything but.)

"Why are you hurting my father?" Esther's voice is that of someone much younger, younger, even, than she was when she first arrived in Massachusetts: it is the voice of a girl who has two parents, and no idea what it is to sit, silent and white-knuckled, through a funeral, and who is afraid of the darkness only because there is no light, and not because she knows what it might conceal.

"Because we can," says the thing. "Because we're hungry, and what's hungry must be fed, don't you think, Esther?" Her name is meat for maggots on the thing's lips. "We're so very, very hungry."

"Run," moans her father again.

"You called us, and we came," says the thing. "This is all for you, Esther. You wished vengeance on those who'd hurt you. You made the proper offerings, gave us blood and tears and so many dearer fluids—all the humors, laid at our gravesites like you knew what you were doing." The thing smiled, showing too many teeth, some with slivers of flesh wedged between them. "Ignorance, as they say, is no defense against the consequences of your actions."

It's an argument a future Esther would have been able to use against the children whose therapists had encouraged them to tell lies about her father, if she hadn't been so shocked and stunned by what was happening around her. This version of Esther will never have the chance, or the need. Her father is bleeding out before her eyes. The things aren't biting him now, but they don't need to be, because the damage is done, and all the regrets in the world won't heal the gashes in his skin.

She's standing in her living room, talking to something out of a nightmare while her father bleeds to death, and she wishes she could make herself believe that this was really happening—or better still, that this was really a dream, and not something she'll have to survive. Right now, she isn't sure she wants to survive.

"People hurt you," says the thing. "People *violated* you. They should never have been allowed to do that. In a just world, they would never have touched you. But there is no justice here. There's just us, and the willingness to do what must be done. To touch, and tear, and rend, and take. We could take you, if you'll come. We could show you what it is to sleep for a hundred years and ride the night on wings of vengeance. We could show you what it is to die, and live forever, and endure. And you would never be hurt again."

Esther stares at her, eyes wide and shining. The thing's words are smooth, cadenced to make her listen. They make promises she's sure can't be kept, but finds herself enthralled by all the same.

A scream pierces the silence they have drawn between them, as high and shrill as the screams of her father when she was still upstairs. This one is even higher, hitting notes that opera divas would envy, shattering and shredding them before racing onward to the next, even higher peak. It's a voice Esther knows better than she knows her own, knows almost better than she knows her father's. She takes a step backward, suddenly cold again, suddenly inescapably sure of one thing: she's not dreaming.

"What *are* you?" she demands.

"We are the dead, and you belong to us now," says the thing.

When she moves, she moves with the supernatural speed of the grave, as swift as a chill racing down the spine, as relentless as the October wind through the leaves. Esther is still, somehow, faster. In this place, in this moment, her feet seem to have wings, and she spins, and runs barefoot down the hall to the kitchen, moving with a speed she has never had before and may never have again, no matter how long she lives—assuming she survives this night. She runs, and behind her, her father's screams split the night...but there's a note of triumph to them now, like he's dying content in the knowledge that his little girl is getting away.

This is the meat of the scenario: this is the place where reality and nightmare collide, healing wounds as old as the psyche itself. Or it would be, had the failsafes not been removed, replaced by a gaping hole into which self and sanity seemed poised to fall. Esther should have been given whispers, rumors, local legends to ease her into the idea that the dead could wake and walk under the right circumstances. She should have been *prepared*, not dropped into a situation that would shred the credibility of anyone who wasn't *there*, who wasn't watching the monsters feed on the flesh of those they loved.

Esther should have been prepared. She should have salt and candle and book and shovel, ready to defend herself, shaped into a warrior by a hundred small, seemingly unrelated incidents. And even that assumes this new, modified situation, and not the harmless haunting Dr. Webb had originally designed for her. Instead, she is barefoot, teenaged, and running for her life, into a night that teems with the hungry dead.

Jennifer isn't screaming anymore by the time Esther reaches the back door. The realization is enough to open a chasm in her chest, deep and terrible and seemingly insurmountable. Her father is dead: she has no question about that. It's strangely easy to accept, like a part of her has been waiting for the universe to realize that it broke up a matched set ever since taking her mother. But if Jennifer is dead, if her best friend is dead, then she's lost everything. She might as well stop running and let the dead take her.

Still, inertia is more powerful than fear, and so her feet keep moving, propelling her onward, through the hole she and Jennifer have carefully cultivated in the fence, into the half-tended yard so similar to her own. The only difference is the sliding glass door at the back of the kitchen, standing already open, letting buttery light spill out into the night air.

There is a body sprawled there. Her heart lurches up into her chest before her eyes finish understanding what they see: a naked man, with skin like gray and polished marble, a knife handle protruding from his open mouth. He's been stabbed clean through the head, but oddly, that doesn't seem to be what killed him. Instinctively, she knows that honor belongs to the salt pooled in his eye sockets, great spoonfuls of salt puddled into mounds atop his face.

There is motion. Jennifer appears, a fireplace poker in one hand and a canister of salt in the other. She's wearing her Bill Nye T-shirt over a pair of yoga pants, and there's a streak of blood down one side of Bill's face, matching the smear of blood on her own cheek. It's a terrible scene. Esther wants to weep for joy.

"You want some?" bellows Jennifer. "You want some, you dead fucks? Because you'll get some!"

Esther wants to tell her not to yell, not to attract more trouble when there's so much trouble already close at hand. All she manages to do is keep running, heedless of the poker, and fling her arms around her best friend's neck, clinging to her like an anchor. Jennifer jumps, stiffens, and manages to recognize Esther before she swings the poker. She doesn't drop it as she closes her arms around the other girl. Her eyes scan the night, over and over, looking for signs of danger, finding them everywhere.

"I thought you were dead," whispers Esther.

"I almost was," says Jennifer. She pulls away, looking Esther assessingly up and down. "Are you hurt?"

Esther's face falls. "My father—"

"My parents too," says Jennifer. There's a brittle bluntness to her that Esther recognizes. Esther falls apart first, gets down to business later. Jennifer is the exact opposite.

For the first time, Esther feels a flicker of hope. If they stay together, they might stand a chance. "How many?"

"Five of them. I killed them all." Jennifer doesn't comment on the nonsensical idea of killing what's already dead, just looks down at the body next to her and delivers a vicious kick to its side, rocking it more securely onto the threshold. "I would have killed a hundred."

"How did you know to use salt?"

"I didn't." For the first time, Jennifer looks faintly embarrassed. The blood on her cheek lends a surreal childishness to her appearance, like she's been caught playing in her fingerpaint for the first time in years. "I was just throwing things, and I threw the salt at one of them, and when it got in his eyes, he fell down and stopped moving. I think it...lays them to rest somehow."

"How much do you have?"

Jennifer lifts her canister, gives it a shake, so that Esther can hear its contents shift. "Not enough," she says grimly. "The street out front is full of them."

So is Esther's yard, and there's no way they won't eventually start coming through the hole in the fence. It would be foolishness to assume any differently. "Okay," she says. "So we run."

THE WOMAN in front of the terminal looked at the screen impassively. The pair of them were doing a surprisingly good job of navigating a scenario with the safeties entirely removed, seeming to know without conscious awareness that if they slipped and died, they would be in trouble. A normal therapeutic revision could involve the death of the subject—Dr. Webb had spoken about the necessity of what she called the "cleansing demise" to drive the point home, and while her research was controversial, no one had been able to disprove its veracity—but only under very carefully controlled circumstances, and only when the chemical balance of the subject had been adjusted to be just *so*.

Under the wrong circumstances, with the wrong chemical cocktail in their veins, subjects could quite literally be frightened to death. An incident which should have been survivable could easily turn fatal, otherwise. If one of the hungry dead—referred to as "revenants" in the project notes, and one of only six types of basic zombie available to the operator—managed to rip out the throat of Dr. Webb's avatar, she might never wake up again. The same went for Esther Hoffman, although the little reporter was a much lower priority. It might even be better if she survived. Truly discredit this facility. Show that nothing good can come of it, and walk away with the research, to continue refining and improving it in private, where no one would be watching.

There was a click from behind her. She didn't turn.

"If you think you've got the nerve to shoot me, shoot me," she said. "If not, run away before I decide this isn't funny anymore. Either way, you might survive. Anything else, you won't."

"Who the fuck are you?"

A male voice this time. She was running out of technicians. With the limited staff currently at the facility, this might be the last she needed to kill. That would be nice. She wasn't getting paid extra for their deaths, and she had never enjoyed freebies.

"My name is irrelevant. If you absolutely must call me something, I believe 'Marline' is still legal in this jurisdiction." She'd burned so many identities over the years that sometimes she couldn't remember which ones were still good, or which ones were absolutely unsafe to use, connecting as they did to deeds which had yet to be attributed to her, things which her employers had paid well to keep off the radar of the general public. "Really, I recommend either shooting or running. You're almost out of time to do either."

She wouldn't still have been talking, had it not been for one simple fact: she knew the person on the other end of the gun wasn't going to shoot her. He sounded too horrified, too unsure. He wasn't a killer. He might be willing to kill to save himself, but once she started moving, he wasn't going to have the opportunity.

The trouble with pursuing this career for so many years was that nothing really surprised her anymore, and hadn't in more than a decade. Employers came and employers went. Jobs were done. If she was good, careful, and lucky, in that order, the work kept coming in, and the money came with it. One day, one of those things would desert her, and she would find herself in the only retirement home offered to people like her—the comfort of the grave. Until then, she would have to work with what she had.

"What did you do?"

She didn't need to see his face to picture it, the horror, the confusion, the revulsion. Really, people were so *dull.* "I killed two of your colleagues, and I'm about to force your employer into a critical synaptic overload. It's going to look like she snapped and killed them herself if I do this correctly, and I always do this correctly. It's going to be beautiful."

"You're here for our research." The horror in his voice was beautiful in its simplicity, briefly overwhelming more squeamish concerns. She felt the brief, inhuman warmth in her abdomen that always accompanied a moment of recognition, of seeing herself in someone else's shadow. This man was no longer troubled by the loss of life, by the fact that two of his colleagues were dead on the ground, unavoidable casualties of the sort of slow war that was more commonly fought in boardrooms and conference centers. He was worried about his research.

Clever man. Reputation and research were two of the things that could endure beyond the flesh, and the flesh was really of minimal consequence: the flesh was weak. The flesh ended. Information went on. Even if it seemed to be forgotten, what was known once would be known forever, in some dusty book, in some dusty room, waiting to be rediscovered.

"Yes, I am." Marline finally turned, standing at the same time, so that she was facing him when she rose.

He was tall, black-haired and brown-skinned, and he frowned at the sight of her, in confusion more than any sort of disapproval. *I've seen you before,* said his expression, and it didn't matter whether he had or not, because he was exactly right and exactly wrong at the same time.

James Bond and Black Widow had long since presented the world with an inaccurate image of the professional spy: poised, perfect, and eminently fuckable, never a hair out of place or a smudge in their lipstick. The sort of person who could wear a tuxedo under a SCUBA array without wrinkling it, who could do backflips in stiletto heels without twisting an ankle. Marline *could* do backflips in heels, if she absolutely had to, but would have been happier eating ground glass. Or simply shooting someone. Shooting someone was almost always the better option.

She was tall, for a woman, with broad shoulders and the sort of soft, rounded build that strangers judged as indolent and her trainers judged as the perfect physique for a weightlifter. Her hands were the only dainty things about her, with long, dexterous fingers that had picked more than their share of locks and cracked more than their share of security codes. She wasn't a thief by trade: leave that to the young and the flexible and the foolish. She was a killer who sometimes took recovery jobs, and knew how to put every ounce of her considerable weight behind a punch.

Her features were plain and pleasant, not entirely eye-catching, capable of being enhanced with the right cosmetics, or played down with the right hairstyle. They had been modified by the virtual world in which Esther and Jennifer were trapped, turned into the best version of themselves, a queen among monsters. Here, in the real world, she was making no such effort. Her tawny brown hair was pulled into a tight bun, and her only concession to vanity was a thin layer of lip gloss, applied when she was still pretending to be a patient. The man in front of her could have seen her a thousand times without consciously registering her presence, and she liked things that way.

What she didn't like was the gun in his hand. She sighed deeply, meeting his eyes. "This could have been accomplished with at least a thin veneer of civility, you know," she said. "You could have chosen to shoot me, or to run. You might even have saved some lives, if you'd run."

"What?" asked the man.

Her kick connected squarely with his wrist, and the uncomfortably wet sound of bones breaking filled the air even as the gun flew from his hand and landed in a pool of congealed blood. He sucked in a breath, clearly intending to scream, and stopped as her fist struck him in the throat, crushing his trachea and silencing him for good. His eyes bulged. He was still clawing at his throat when she slashed it open, releasing his last breath in a hissing sigh that was tidily drowned out by the hot red rush of blood.

"I do regret this," she said, as he dropped to his knees on the floor. "Honestly, I'm not being paid nearly enough for the amount of killing I've felt compelled to do since I got here. You represent a professional failing."

The bleeding man, clutching at his throat, said nothing.

"You wouldn't have needed to die if your boss had simply been willing to acquiesce to reasonable requests for investment opportunities. I hope you're aware of that. This is entirely your Dr. Webb's fault, and when you see her in the afterlife, you should give her a piece of your mind."

The man collapsed, no longer clutching at his throat, no longer doing anything. Marline prodded his body with her foot. He didn't move.

"Right," she said.

The room was a disaster: no one who walked down the hall would be able to miss the fact that something bad had happened here, even if they weren't close enough to see the bodies. The drive she had attached to the main terminal was still blinking as it transferred data. These were secure files measured in terabytes. Even with the best equipment money could buy—and hers *was* the best equipment money could buy—she still needed time to get things done.

"I will have my bonus or I will have your head," she muttered, and closed the door. Let the remaining staffers raise a hue and cry. It wouldn't slow her down any further than their pointless interruptions, and she was nearly done here. She just needed a little more time.

A little more time, and to finish her secondary objective. Marline walked back to what she had come to think of as "her" chair and settled, reaching for the keyboard. It was time to finish this.

___ 6. Confrontation.

ESTHER AND Jennifer flee hand in hand down the street, both still in their pajamas, neither of them looking back. Bits of rock and gravel bite the soles of their feet, making Esther regret that they left so fast that neither of them stopped to scavenge for shoes. They had no choice. There were noises from her backyard and from the cemetery beyond the fence, making it quietly obvious that time is running out. So they ran, and they're still running, still together, fleeing an impossible fate.

Survival matters more than a few scrapes and bruises. Survival, and staying together. They're both orphans now, and if they had the breath to speak or the ability to form a coherent thought about anything beyond survival, they would be apologizing to each other, grieving with each other. Instead, they're reduced to living with each other, and that may be the most painful thing of all. They have to keep on living.

Esther runs and knows that she can run forever, as long as Jennifer is with her; as long as she isn't facing this, or anything else, alone. If they stay together, she'll survive.

Jennifer runs and knows she can't run forever: that her body will eventually betray her, that her fear of failure will overwhelm her ability to keep on moving, that she doesn't have Esther's experience with loss, or Esther's faith. Esther believes in her. She's always known that, and been happy to take quiet advantage of it, painting herself as the ringleader in their little circus of two. But now, there's no one for her to lean on, and if Esther leans too hard, she's going to topple over.

They need a miracle. They need a rescue. They're unlikely to find either.

Lights are on all up and down the street. Doors are kicked open, windows are smashed, and the screams, when they come, are agonized and short-lived. The dead are mostly inside, for now, filling their bellies on the living. When the living are exhausted, however, the dead will return. The girls know that, as surely as they know that their only hope sits at the end of the block, in a rainbow haze of neon lights and two-for-one hot dogs.

The convenience store door is closed when they arrive. The lights are on, and Jennifer glimpses the terrified face of Daphne, still in her vampire makeup, between two advertisements for cigarettes. She runs a little faster, towing Esther along with her, and slams her fists against the door. The salt she's still holding makes it difficult, but this whole night has been difficult; what's one thing more? Esther backs up a step, both hands wrapped around the baseball bat, scanning the parking lot for danger.

Baseball bat? The question is small and confused, originating at the back of her mind. *Wasn't it a fireplace poker a moment ago?*

(In another place, in another time, in a world that might as well not have existed, Marline swore quietly and made an adjustment to the program, fixing the brief glitch that had caused some elements to be overwritten by the defaults. She couldn't bring back the poker without drawing attention, but she could keep

things from shifting further. The temptation to dial up the insta-
bility to eleven—to change the weakness of the walking dead
from salt to pepper, or mustard, or something even less logi-
cal—was strong. She resisted it. If the program became "unfair,"
unwilling to adhere to its own logic, it could trigger fail safes she
lacked the ability to disconnect, kicking Esther and Jennifer out
of their pods with their minds and memories intact. No. They
had to play this out to its conclusion, while she ramped both the
lethality of the scenario and the levels of psychotropic chemicals
in their blood through the roof. They wouldn't be walking away
from this. Of that, she was absolutely sure.)

"Let us *in*, you asshole!" howls Jennifer, and hits the door
again. Daphne gives her a terrified look, hanging back with the
others already in the store. None of Daphne's usual gang seem to
be there. They must not have made it.

Under other circumstances, Jennifer might have been willing
to stop and feel sorry for her, even if only for a moment. Losing a
friend is a terrible thing, after all. But Jennifer is trapped outside,
and so is *her* best friend, her gang, who isn't dead yet. They need
to be in that store.

"We know how to stop them!" she shouts, mouth as close to
the glass as she can manage. Esther backs toward her, their shoulders bumping. Jennifer stiffens but doesn't turn. She knows what
she'll see. She doesn't want to see it. Not before she has to. So she
hits the glass again, and yells, "Come on, you fucking cowards! Let
us in! We need to stop them!"

Daphne says something to the others. Jennifer can't hear her,
but the shape of the word on Daphne's lips is familiar, and Jennifer
almost laughs when she realizes what it is: egghead. Daphne is
saying that the egghead usually knows what she's talking about.

Daphne, who caused all of this, who drove them into the dark, into the place where the dead things waited, is going to save them.

It's a gawky late shift employee who unlocks the door, face so pale that his acne scars stand out like brands. He re-locks it again behind them, and Jennifer finally turns, finally sees the swarm of the hungry dead walking with calm, placid inevitability into the parking lot. This is the place, then. This is where they make their last stand.

Some of the fear drains out of her. She and Esther, they're both here. If they live to see tomorrow, they'll have to admit that they're alone in the world now, but for tonight, they're still together, they're still standing. They can do this.

She turns to the spot-faced boy. "We need all the salt you have," she says. "Rock salt, commercial salt, even those stupid little packets you put next to the hot dogs. Salt kills them."

"How do you know that?" Daphne asks. Her voice quavers at the beginning of the sentence, but by the end, she seems to be finding some of her old confidence. The high school pecking order lives on, at least in Daphne's mind. Without nerds, she wasn't a popular girl, because what is popularity without something to compare it to? Now the nerds are here, and she's better than them again. All is right with the world.

Well. Except for the monsters outside, the ones who killed her friends and her little brother and her parents. But those are probably here because of something the nerds did. That's the way monsters work, isn't it? They show up because the nerds did something wrong.

"Is this your fault?" Daphne demands.

"No," says Esther. Her voice is low, half-swallowed, almost wiped away by the angle of her chin, which is pointed down toward her chest as she tries to catch her breath. She never runs that much. Still, she finds the strength to raise her head, one agonizing inch at a time, until she's staring directly at Daphne. "This is *your* fault."

Daphne recoils. It feels like every eye is suddenly on her, and not in the way that she prefers. "What are you talking about?"

"You and your friends. This is your fault."

"You *assholes*," snarls Jennifer. She has a target for her anger now. The dead are outside, and she can hate them—oh, how she can hate them—but she can't be angry at them the way she can be angry at a human being. It's hard to be angry at what feels like an act of God. "You just had to show that you were better than us, didn't you? You just had to play fuck with the geeks. So you chased us into a fucking *curse*, and now the dead are walking, and this is *all your fault*."

A murmur passes through the other survivors in the convenience store. Daphne looks increasingly uncomfortable. She has nowhere to run. Anyone who looks at their situation can tell that, easily. If the crowd turns on her, she's dead.

"You can't really blame me," she says. "It was a joke."

"You broke one of my teeth," says Jennifer.

"It was a *joke*," insists Daphne. "It just got...it just got a little out of hand."

Silence falls over the store, restless and uneasy and filled with the potential for violence. Jennifer turns back to the clerk.

"We need salt," she says. "Fast. We don't have time for this."

She's saved Daphne's place in the store with her intercession and she knows it. So does Daphne. Esther watches as the former vampire queen fades back into the crowd, eyes glossy with shock and fear, skin the slightest bit too pale. If they all survive this night, Daphne's power will have been broken. Her reign is over.

The clerk nods and leads Jennifer into the shelves, and Esther relaxes, ever so slightly. They have a chance. They'll have salt, and they'll have a chance. If they can make it until morning, if they can stay alive, they can survive this. They can walk away.

Something hits the glass. There is a smashing sound. Esther turns. Daphne screams.

One of the hungry dead has punched a hole in the window, and is reaching for them. He'll widen that opening soon, if he's allowed. Esther raises her baseball bat, ready to swing, only to fall back as Jennifer charges past her, a canister of salt in each hand, the spouts open and ready to pour.

"Get the fuck away from her!" she howls, scattering salt in all directions. When it hits the dead man's eyes he falls backward, collapsing like the corpse he is.

Jennifer stops, catching her breath, and turns to beam smugly at Esther. "See?" she says. "You're going to be fine. We're going to be fine. As long as we're together, you're going to be okay. I—"

She never sees the hands that grab her from behind, jerking her through the hole, out into the night.

But she feels the teeth. Oh, she feels the teeth. The last thing she hears is Esther screaming, followed by nothing.

Nothing.

NOTHING.

Dr. Jennifer Webb opened her eyes on darkness, and the sound of an alarm shrieking high and shrill somewhere in the distance, warning of an impending systems failure. Her limbs felt like they were made of lead, and her head was pounding wildly, almost drowning out the din. Worst of all was the pain in her chest, a squeezing, compressing feeling that made it almost impossible to breathe.

I'm having a heart attack, she thought, dazed. Another thought came close on the heels of the first: *I can't be having a heart attack. I'm too young to be having a heart attack.* Her father liked to tell her that she was going to eat herself into an early grave, while her mother always insisted that she was big-boned like her grandmother and would settle into her own skin one day. Either way, sixteen is too young for a heart attack, and—

Wait. Sixteen? She hadn't been sixteen in years.

Phase slipping. Shit. That was a consequence of bad scenario management. They'd seen it a lot in the beginning, people emerging from the pods with a bad case of the mental bends, unable to distinguish the scenarios they'd just lived through from the world they were coming home to. Since the changes wrought by the scenarios were designed to be permanent, deeply shaping the psyche, it made sense: the mind needed time to adjust. Her mind needed time to adjust.

Time is not a thing she has right now. Slipping back into the dreamlike present tense state of the scenario is easy—too easy. The drugs weren't cleared out of her system properly before the pod woke her, and she's flying, soaring on a pharmaceutical tide. The pain in her chest isn't getting any better, and if she doesn't do something soon, it's going to kill her. She knows that. She knows that, and still she can't move.

Esther, she thinks suddenly. The name is accompanied by a rush of serotonin, love and loyalty and fear and concern all mixed into a potent natural cocktail that is, miraculously, strong enough to let her rock onto her side in the limited space provided by the pod. She can't remember the code to get out, can barely remember where she *is*, but muscle memory is sometimes stronger than mental memory, and when she raises her shaking hand to the keypad, her fingers know what to do.

There is a hiss, and the pod swings open, allowing the colder air from the lab to flow inside. It strikes—struck—Jennifer across the face, slapping her back into the slower, calmer tempo of the real world. Slowly, with shaking hands, she disconnected the sensors from her body and half-slid, half-tumbled out of the pod, rolling clean off the edge of the table to land on the floor with a painful, bone-shaking thud. Even that pain wasn't as bad as the throbbing in her chest, which kept getting bigger and bigger, seeming to take up the entire world.

This isn't a true heart attack, she thought, doing her best to ignore the steady "because I'm too young for that" beating at the back of her mind. Pushing herself onto hands and knees, she crawled toward the wall, and the emergency response kit. Her heart wasn't going out of sync because of any innate damage. She had no history of hypertension or heart disease, despite her father's dire predictions about her weight. This was all shock. This was only shock. This was something she could stop. This was something she *had* to stop, because Esther's pod was still closed, and the scenario that had just killed her had been far more dire than it was supposed to have been.

Dimly, she remembered dialing Esther into a scenario set at a middle school, where the darkest enemy she should have faced was a much younger, less violent Daphne. Someone had modified the scenario. They hadn't been prepared for that, mentally, pharmaceutically, to go that deep. No wonder her mind and body were both in open rebellion. They had been put through something they hadn't been prepared for.

The situation flickers back into the present tense as she drags her way across the floor. She doesn't fight it. In the present tense, she's still more than half the brave teenager who dies saving her best friend from an impossible foe. In the present tense, she can do anything, if anything will mean saving Esther.

Hand over hand, she drags herself, until the first aid kit is only inches away. The pain in her chest pulses, intensifies, and takes the world away, with Jennifer fighting it all the way down.

MARLINE SIGHED as Jennifer Webb stopped moving. It was almost a pity. The woman had fought so hard, and had almost been able to make it. Ah, well. Maintaining a perfect record meant a lot of people had to die, no matter how hard they tried to fight.

The drive beeped. The data transfer was finally finished; everything had been pulled down from the cloud storage and out of the facility hardware, and she could go. Really, despite the extra deaths, this day had gone better than she could possibly have asked. The data was secure. The doctor was down. Whether the reporter lived or not was irrelevant, because she had no idea of the events that had transpired outside her pod.

It took less than a minute to disconnect the drive and secure it inside her jacket. The scenario was still running; a glance at the screen showed her a small band of survivors on the roof of the convenience store, scattering salt in all directions as they struggled to stay alive. No time to stay and watch Hoffman die.

It was a pity, really. What was a horror movie without a gory and cathartic ending?

Profitable, that was what. The data she had stolen was going to make her even more comfortably wealthy than she already was, and the fact that she had been able to perform this trick in the face of tight security—lax once she was inside, but getting in had been the trick—would bring still more work her way. This was the sort of job she lived for. A hard shell, a soft center, and all the profit in the world.

Stepping over the body in the middle of the floor, she walked calmly to the door and pulled it open. Then she stopped, cocking her head to the side.

"Ah," she said finally. "I suppose you're not dead after all."

Dr. Jennifer Webb, holding the doorframe with one hand to steady herself, holding the empty syringe of epinephrine in her other hand, glared. "Who the *fuck* are you?" she snarled.

"I am an independent contractor," said Marline, and punched her in the throat—or tried to. Dr. Webb wasn't there anymore.

Dr. Webb, the thirty-seven year old scientist with no athletic tendencies, who worked out only when she had absolutely no choice, had dodged. Marline blinked. Then, delighted, she laughed.

"You have a younger woman's reflexes," she said, delighted. "Your psychological changes carry over into the physiological. Oh, that's a rich surprise. How long do the effects last? Have they been documented?"

Dr. Webb responded by snarling and stabbing her in the arm with the empty syringe.

Marline's expression never changed. "That was a mistake," she said, before grabbing Dr. Webb by the forearms and using her leverage to fling the other woman into the bloody abattoir of the observation room. Dr. Webb landed with a squawk and a thud, unable to get her feet back under herself. Marline stalked after her, producing a fishing knife from inside her coat.

"Hurts more this way," she said, and drove it into Dr. Webb's belly.

Jennifer Webb had experienced pain in her life, but never like this, never like a firework going off in a dark sky, so bright and violent that it eclipsed everything else. Even the lingering ache from her abortive heart attack and the needle she had shoved into her own chest was pushed to the side, chased away by the agony of the stab wound. Her eyes went wide.

"Guk," she said, small and tight in the back of her throat.

"Yes," said Marline, letting go of the blade. "Perhaps you should have chosen a less dangerous career."

"Uck," said Jennifer, even smaller, even tighter, the sound dwindling even as it was made.

Marline smiled as she turned to go, and found herself nose-to-nose with Esther Hoffman.

Esther didn't speak. Esther didn't flinch. She brought the scalpel she had stolen from the medication prep station in the hall up in a swift arc, slicing across Marline's throat in a single concussive motion. Blood erupted from the opening in a hot red geyser, spraying everywhere, liberally coating Esther in the stuff. Esther didn't blink.

(*blood is nothing blood is nothing new blood is already everywhere; when she blinks, blood is everywhere, she went after Jennifer, she went to save Jennifer, and she woke up in a strange white place surrounded by machines and her body is too long and too slow but it doesn't matter, because she was covered in blood just a few seconds ago and now she's covered in blood again and this is only right this is only right this is the world setting itself right again)*

Marline did blink, several times, shocked and pained and unable to believe what was happening to her. Then, without any fanfare, she fell backward, into the blood. She landed next to the body of the last technician she had killed.

Esther dropped the scalpel and ran to Jennifer's side, dropping to her knees in the soupy mess. Jennifer's eyes were rolling wildly, and her breaths were coming short and sharp, like she no longer quite remembered how breathing was supposed to go.

"Jennifer? Jennifer! Don't die. Don't leave me again." Esther moved so that her friend's head was in her lap, stroking her hair. She didn't touch the knife. It scared her. There was too much danger in it, barely contained, begging to break free. Instead, she folded herself forward, around her friend, like she could protect her. "Don't die."

The world is wobbling around her, shifting from strangely solid to waving and dreamlike so quickly that her head spins. She doesn't know where she is or how she got there or why her body feels so wrong, but she knows this is Jennifer (even if she looks older, worn down, strange), and she knows she has to protect her.

"Don't die," she whispers again, and closes her eyes, and waits for a miracle.

___ 7. Miraculous.

"IT'S A miracle I survived," said Dr. Jennifer Webb. She was sitting at prim attention, naturally good posture improved and encouraged by the healing stab wound in her belly. "The doctors were able to counteract the sepsis, although I lost nearly a foot of intestine."

"A miracle—or a problem?" The interviewer leaned forward, expression schooled into one of studious concern. "There have been several lawsuits brought against your institute—"

"All of which have been dismissed. The people claiming mental damage knew what they were risking when they chose our treatment plan, and we're still helping far more than we could ever have harmed." Dr. Webb shook her head. "The intruder modified the running scenario so dramatically that the chemical combination we were using to balance the brain chemistry of the subjects couldn't possibly keep up. They were trying to cause permanent damage. Our normal therapies don't carry half that much risk. The people who have filed lawsuits against us were trying to profit off a tragedy, not responding to tragedies of their own."

"So you've said, but you know I have to ask. Has Esther Hoffman brought suit against you?"

Ah: there was the sting. Dr. Webb forced a smile. "No. Miss Hoffman is recuperating from her ordeal, but has expressed no interest in suing the institute."

"She hasn't been seen since you were both released from the hospital."

"She has provided proof of life whenever asked. Please, respect her privacy, and mine, during these trying times."

The interview from there followed the usual lines: questions about her work, about the people who might have been trying to steal it away from her, about where she was intending to take it next. Dr. Webb answered them all as best she could, and managed to hide her relief when it was over until she was no longer anywhere near a camera.

She was learning.

◁▷

"ESTHER! I'M home!"

The living room of their small colonial home was silent, but that was normal. Esther didn't usually leave her room when there was no one else in the house, preferring to sit by the window and watch for signs that they were about to be attacked. No sooner was the door shut than Esther came pounding down the stairs, hitting them each as hard as she had when she was sixteen and had no weakness in her ankles or concern about falling.

Jennifer lit up at the sight of her, and let go of the overlay of her adult self, which she had been—has been—struggling to hold in place since she left the house this morning. It's so much easier to relax into the seamless "now" of the teenage self her equipment created. The one her equipment can't unmake. Too many shocks, too many stresses—it will be years before she can find a way to delete the ghosts of a past she never had from her conscious mind. If she even chooses to go back. She may be an echo of a girl who never lived, but that doesn't mean she wants to die. Not when she's finally alive.

Not when Esther needs her.

Esther had been the primary target of the scenario, and she doesn't have the luxury of choosing. There's too much damage; it runs too deep. She dreams the adult version of herself, but she always wakes up crying, aware that what she's seen from a shattered distance has been lost forever, burned away by the effort of breaking free, of getting to Jennifer. To save her friend, she sacrificed herself. She doesn't mind, though. She has her sketchbooks, and the whole internet to discover, hundreds of movies and television shows and books that seem to have been tailored to exactly her tastes (curated by an adult self she has abandoned), and best of all, most of all, she has Jennifer.

As long as she has Jennifer, she'll be fine.

They embrace in the middle of the room, two teenage girls who never existed, out of place and out of time and finally back where they feel like they belong, and everything is just the way they want it to be. When they let each other go, they continue holding hands, and they walk, the risen dead of their own past selves, onward toward the trembling and uncertain future.